PURCHASED FROM
MULTNOMAH COUNTY LIBRARY
TITLE WAVE BOOKSTORE

Behind the Eyes of Dreamers
and Other Short Novels

Behind the Eyes of Dreamers and Other Short Novels

Pamela Sargent

Five Star • Waterville, Maine

Copyright © 2002 by Pamela Sargent
Introduction copyright © 2002 by George Zebrowski.

"Shadows," copyright © 1974 by Terry Carr. First appeared in *Fellowship of the Stars*, edited by Terry Carr (Simon & Schuster). Copyright reassigned to the author in 1977.
"Behind the Eyes of Dreamers," copyright © 1990 by TSR, Inc. First appeared in *Amazing Stories*, November 1990.
"The Renewal," copyright © 1978 by Jack Dann. First appeared in *Immortal: Short Novels of the Transhuman Future*, edited by Jack Dann (Harper & Row).

The above short novels are reprinted here by permission of the author and her agents, Richard Curtis Associates, Inc., 171 East 74th Street, New York, NY 10021.

All rights reserved.

This collection is a work of fiction. Names, characters, places, and incidents are either the product of the author's imagination, or, if real, used fictitiously.

Five Star First Edition Science Fiction and Fantasy Series.

Published in 2002 in conjunction with Tekno Books
and Ed Gorman.

Set in 11 pt. Plantin by Minnie B. Raven.

Printed in the United States on permanent paper.

Library of Congress Cataloging-in-Publication Data

Sargent, Pamela.
    Behind the eyes of dreamers and other short novels / Pamela Sargent.
        p. cm.—(Five Star first edition science fiction and fantasy series)
    Contents: Shadows—Behind the eyes of dreamers—The renewal.
    ISBN 0-7862-3879-8 (hc : alk. paper)
    1. Science fiction, American.   I. Title.   II. Series.
PS3569.A6887 B44 2002
    813'.54—dc21   2001055737

To Martin H. Greenberg and John Helfers,
riders to the rescue more than once

Table of Contents

Introduction by George Zebrowski   9

Shadows   15

Behind the Eyes of Dreamers   62

The Renewal   131

Introduction

by George Zebrowski

The time is now long past when I have to worry about repeating the vast praise given to Pamela Sargent for her work from critics and reviewers, and from sources as diverse as Michael Bishop, Gahan Wilson, Gregory Benford, James Morrow, Harlan Ellison, and George Alec Effinger. If I extended this list, I would have no room in this introduction for anything else. They all say what I have always known—that Pamela Sargent is one of the best living writers of any kind.

Although for many years she was not even nominated for a single award, and has been the subject of laughably misguided reviews, it was a continued sign of her influence and acceptance that she was long believed to have been nominated for and won awards. I had listened to writers complain in her company that they had never won an award, despite having been nominated often, and watched their jaws drop when she calmly told them that she had never been on a final ballot. This, of course, kept her out of membership in "the Nebula Award losers club," which she cannot join even today, because she won when she was nominated for the first time.

She was nominated for and won other awards in the 1990s, and the praise continues at a high level; but Pamela Sargent does not promote herself and belongs to no clique. She finds asking another writer for a jacket comment distasteful. She has never attended a writing workshop. At one time this was thought to be shyness on her part, but the shyness was only the superficial sign of something deeper and stronger—an individualism that has always known that in matters of achievement we must all stand alone. No one can write the story or novel for you; no one can see, feel, and think as you do; and this individuality is all that an artist has to offer. Dilute it with too many other voices and that uniqueness is destroyed. Too many human activities are imitative and unnecessary in their repetitiveness. Likewise, activities that make the garnering of praise an overly collective, political skill, risk the reward of overpraise, even of lies.

Sargent's prose style reflects her sturdy individualism. Electric currents of feeling and thought flow through her stories, sometimes overwhelming readers who expect something more amiable; but whether they like the work or not, they are not likely to forget it. Sargent opens up human hearts as few writers of science fiction have ever done, and she does so with a spare, flinty, gritty, sometimes nervous prose that does not tolerate the lazy reader.

She is one of the few writers who has the arrayed strengths of thought, feeling, and technical skill to do justice to genuine, knowledge-based science fictional themes, to what some people call hard science fiction. This is a great rarity, since the ability to think through subtle ideas, to always be able to ask the next question, does not work well with the skills of characterization and writerly prose. The sheer dazzle of ideas is diminished without the equally intriguing human impact of future possibilities. A writer who can march through a reader's mind on all these fronts at once is at least knocking at the doors of greatness.

Sargent, with her counter-melodramatic, Greek tragedian's restraint, confronts the reader with the human consequences of future changes. She is neither technophobe nor technophile, or ideologue. There is wonder in her stories, but no easy fantasy or wish-fulfillment. To know her characters is to suffer with them and to exult over their victories (when a victory is possible). It is difficult to guess how a Sargent story or novel will grow, and that is part of how she generates suspense. Readers have reported that reading her is always an experience so convincing, rich and nourishing of thought and understanding, that they believe the author had somehow managed to experience the events in her story.

Many of Sargent's earlier novels demand to be rediscovered, especially *The Golden Space*, the technical adroitness of which is surprisingly illustrated by its opening section, "The Renewal," written and published as a separate piece long before the novel, and included in this collection in its original form.

Her Venus trilogy, recently completed, is essential to an appreciation of modern science fiction. Gregory Benford wrote about the opening volume, *Venus of Dreams*, that it is "a sensitive portrait of people caught up in a vast project. It tells us about how people react to technology's relentless hand, and does so deftly. A new high point in humanistic science fiction." And about the second volume, *Venus of Shadows*, he wrote that "the sway of worlds and human masses does not cloak the personal tales that Sargent follows with a patient, insightful eye. Here humanity is aware that science has given it stewardship over all life, bringing a subtle, somber weight to even coffee-klatch gossip."

Child of Venus, Sargent's most recent novel and the completion of her Venus trilogy, elicited varied favorable reactions. Donald M. Hassler wrote in *The New York Review of*

Science Fiction that for some writers "the stylistic and narrative experiments of the great modernist James Joyce have been an inspiration; and now we might include Pamela Sargent in that group, although she satisfies our genre expectations as well . . . Sargent's accomplishment here is superb." And Kilian Melloy, of wigglefish.com, sums it up by saying that "Sargent transcends genre and achieves something rare in the world of letters: a genuine contemplation of truth, in all its nasty, brilliant glory."

Reviewers also pointed out the uniform high quality and dedicated purpose of the trilogy. We see this inability to fall below high ambition in all of Sargent's work.

An earlier novel, *The Shore of Women*, was praised for its "luminous prose and vivid characters" in a "compelling and emotionally involving novel." It has been given the sincerest form of flattery: swift imitation.

Sargent's historical novel about the life of Genghis Khan, *Ruler of the Sky*, has revealed her as an historical novelist of the first rank. It received the kind of praise that most writers can only dream about. The late great Gary Jennings, author of *Aztec* and many other historical novels, wrote that "This formidably researched and exquisitely written novel is surely destined to be known hereafter as *the* definitive history of the life and times and conquests of Genghis, mightiest of Khans." And Elizabeth Marshall Thomas, the anthropologist and author of *Reindeer Moon*, declared, "I love it . . . the book is fascinating from cover to cover."

Sargent's alternative historical companion novel to *Ruler of the Sky*, *Climb The Wind*, was described by Gahan Wilson as bringing "a new dimension to the form," and by other reviewers as "a triumph," and as a "complex and masterful" animation of characters "who demand our sympathy and affection."

I could go on for a hundred pages. Despite the failure of publishers, the overwhelmingly favorable reaction of readers, critics, and reviewers of every stripe, is unavoidable.

I've described Pamela Sargent's work from a reader's point of view; but I've also observed her editorially, and as a fellow writer. And what I have seen happen over the years is the growth of a vehement talent finding its own way, as I've had to find mine. Something awesome has come to life within my beloved companion. To see this happen in a human being in whom I have also known frailties and faults is doubly impressive.

The other two short novels included with "The Renewal" in this collection, the Conradian "Behind the Eyes of Dreamers," and the Terry Carr-encouraged "Shadows," are both rarities, difficult to find in their original incarnations. I am glad to see them all in one volume, and I envy the new readers who will see these novellas for the first time.

When I read a new story or novel by Pamela Sargent, I forget that I write. She sometimes comes into the room and distracts me. Then I tell the intruding mortal to leave, so I can read the writer.

George Zebrowski
October 1, 2001

George Zebrowski is the author of some 35 books and hundreds of stories and essays, as well as the editor of many anthologies. His novel *Brute Orbits* won the John W. Campbell Award for best science fiction novel of the year.

Shadows

The sun hid its face behind the clouds, a gray layered curtain which hung close to the Earth. Defeated, the city's inhabitants trudged along the highway, crowding the four lanes. Suzanne Molitieri could hear the droning of murmurs punctuated by an occasional wail. *Don't look back.* She kept her eyes resolutely focused on the asphalt at her feet as she walked. Her hand clutched Joel's, both palms dry. Around her, people twisted their necks as they glanced back at the empty city.

Above them silver insects hovered, humming softly and casting faint shadows over the people below. They were passing the suburbs now and more people joined the stream, trickling down the highway entrances, creating small eddies before becoming part of the river. *Herded like animals.* Suzanne glanced at Joel, saw his brown eyes focused on her, and grasped his hand more tightly.

Resistance had been futile. A few invaders had been slaughtered by gunfire in Buenos Aires as they left their ship, and Buenos Aires had vanished, people and all. When the same thing happened in Canton and Washington, the will to resist had subsided. Suzanne doubted that it had completely vanished.

The Earth was an anthill to the Aadae. They had descended on it from the skies, stepping on it here and there when it was necessary. Yet Suzanne had seen an Aada in the city streets weeping over the dead burned bodies of some who had resisted. Then she and the others had been herded from the city, allowed to take nothing with them but the clothes they wore and a few personal possessions. Suzanne carried more clothes in a knapsack. She had left everything else behind; the past would be of no use to her now. Joel carried a pound of marijuana and some bottles of liquor in his knapsack; he was already planning for the future.

Suzanne adjusted the burden on her back. Around her the murmuring died and she heard only the sound of feet marching, treading the pavement with soft thuds. The conquered people moved past the rows of suburban houses which were silent witnesses to the procession.

Suzanne thought of empty turtle shells. The gunmetal gray domes surrounded her, covering the countryside in uneven rows. Groups of people huddled in front of each dome, waiting passively. She thought of burial mounds.

"How they get them up so fast?" A stocky black man standing near her was looking at a dome. He began to rub his hand across its gray surface. Suzanne could hear the sound of weeping. A plump pale woman next to Joel was whimpering, clinging to a barrel-chested man who was probably her husband.

"They took her kids away," a voice said. Suzanne found herself facing a slender black woman with hazel eyes. The woman's hair was coiled tightly around her head in cornrow braids. "She had six of them," the black woman went on. "They took them all to some other domes."

Suzanne, not knowing what to say, looked down at her feet, then back at the woman. "Did you have kids too?" she asked lamely.

"No, I always wanted to, but I'm glad now I didn't." The woman smiled bitterly and Suzanne felt that the subject was being dismissed. The stocky black man had wandered to the dome's triangular entrance. "I'm Felice Harrison," the woman muttered. "That's my husband Oscar." She waved at the man in the entrance.

"I'm Suzanne Molitieri." The introduction hung in the air between them. Suzanne wanted to giggle suddenly. Felice raised her eyebrows slightly.

"Are you all right?"

"I'm fine," said Suzanne, almost squeaking the words. Oscar joined his wife and placed his arm gently over her shoulders.

"This is Suzanne Molitieri," Felice said to Oscar, and Suzanne felt reassured by the steady smile on the man's broad face.

"I'm Joel Feldstein," Joel said quickly, and she felt his hand close around her waist. She had almost forgotten he was there. His hand seemed as heavy as a chain, binding her to him.

Joel smiled. His too-perfect teeth seemed to glitter; his brown eyes danced. With his free hand, he brushed back a lock of thick brown hair. *He's too beautiful—I had to love him.* "I guess we're going to live in these things," Joel continued. "I can't figure it out, I don't understand these people. That's quite an admission for me; I've studied psychology for years. In fact, I was finishing my doctoral studies." *You haven't been near a classroom in years.* "I wanted to go into research, then marry Suzanne, give her a chance to finish school; she's been working much too hard helping me out." He smiled down at her regretfully. *Somebody had to pay the bills.* "The thing I regret most is not getting the chance to help Suzie." She winced at the nickname. The chainlike pressure on her waist tightened. "What about you two, what did you do?"

"It hardly matters now," Felice said dryly. Her hazel

eyes and Oscar's black ones were expressionless.

"I guess you're right," said Joel. "You know, I even had a couple of papers published last year—I was really proud of that—but I guess that doesn't matter now either." *Why are you lying now?*

"I was a bus driver," said Oscar coldly. Suzanne suddenly felt that she was looking at the Harrisons across an abyss. Her mind began to clutch at words in desperation.

"What's it like inside the dome?" she said to Oscar. The black man seemed to relax slightly.

"Just a big room, with low tables and no chairs," Oscar answered. "Then there's these metal stairways winding around, and some rooms without doors, and the ceiling's glowing, don't ask me how. No lights, just this glow."

"Hey," Felice muttered. The people around them had formed a line. Suzanne turned. One of the Aadae stood in front of them, holding a small metal device.

Suzanne sniffed at the air. She hadn't realized how smelly the Aadae actually were. She watched the alien and wondered again how the military must have felt when they first saw the conquerors.

The Aada appeared human, a small female not more than five feet tall and slender, with large violet eyes and pale golden skin. Her blue-black hair, uncombed and apparently unwashed, hung to her waist. She wore a dirty pair of bikini bottoms, spotted with stains. The alien scratched her stomach, and Suzanne almost snickered.

"Give nameh, go inside," said the Aada. She waved the metal rod she held at the dome. Then she pointed it at Joel. "Give nameh, go inside." The Aada's violet eyes stared past them, as if perceiving something else besides the line of people.

"Joel Feldstein." The rod was pointed at Suzanne.
"Suzanne Molitieri."
"Oscar Harrison."
"Felice Harrison." They began to move toward the dome.

"Are my children all right, please tell me, are they all right?" The plump mother of six was pleading with the alien.

"Nameh," the Aada repeated. Suzanne looked into the alien's violet eyes and was startled to see sadness there. The Aada's small golden hand patted the plump woman reassuringly. "Nameh," and the word this time seemed tinged by grief.

Puzzled, Suzanne turned away and entered the dome.

"You tell me," said Joel, "how a technologically advanced culture can produce such sloppy, dirty people. I can't get within two feet of one." He grimaced.

"Cleanliness and technological advancement aren't necessarily related," said Gabe Cardozo, shifting his plump body around on the floor. "Besides, from their point of view, they might be very neat. It depends on your perspective."

Suzanne, huddled against the wall near the doorless entrance to their room, suddenly felt dizzy. They had been drinking from one of Joel's bottles since early that evening. She tried to focus on the wall opposite the entrance.

The room was bare of furnishings except for two mats on the floor. A small closet near the door held their possessions. There was little space to move around in and she knew they were lucky to have the room to themselves. Gabe, two domes down, was sharing his room with three other people. She had asked Joel if they could have Gabe move in with them; he was, after all, Joel's best friend. But Joel had dismissed the idea, saying he had little enough privacy as it was. *No, you have to hide, Joel, that's it, Gabe might find out what you really are.*

"What do they want, anyway?" said Joel. "They took the trouble to put up these domes, I don't know how, moved us in, and we've been sitting around for three days with nothing to do." Joel suddenly laughed. "Whoever thought an alien invasion would be so goddamn boring."

"Well, they obviously don't need slave labor," Gabe said. "They put up these domes with no help and they are technologically advanced. And if they'd wanted the planet for themselves, I suppose they could have executed us. They want us for something, and they probably moved us out here so they could watch us more carefully. People could hide in the city."

"What difference does it make?" Suzanne said loudly, irritated by Gabe's professorial manner. "We'll find out sooner or later; what good does it do talking about it?" She stood up, wobbling a bit on weak-kneed legs. Gabe's walruslike moustache seemed to droop slightly; Joel shrugged his shoulders.

She found herself outside the room on the metal stairway, leaning forward, clutching the rail. The large room below her was empty and someone had pushed the low tables closer to the walls. She began to move down the stairs, still holding the rail. When she reached the bottom, she sat down abruptly on the floor, clutching her knees. "God," she whispered. The floor shifted under her.

A hand was on her shoulder. Startled, she looked up into Felice's hazel eyes. "Are you all right?"

"I'm fine," said Suzanne. "I don't know. I think I'm going to vomit."

"You need some air, come on." Suzanne stumbled to her feet. Holding on to Felice, she managed to get to the triangular doorway and outside.

A cool breeze bathed her face. "You better now?" asked Felice.

"I think so." She looked at the rows of lighted doorways in front of her. "You're up pretty late, Felice."

"I'm up pretty early. It's almost morning." Suzanne sighed and leaned against the dome. "You feel like taking a walk, honey?"

"Can we?" asked Suzanne. "Will they let us?"

"They haven't stopped me yet. No wonder you look so bad, staying inside for three days. Come on, we can walk to the highway; do you good."

"All right." Her head felt clearer already. She began to walk past the rows of domes with Felice. Occasionally, shadows moved across the triangular doorways they passed, transforming themselves into loose-limbed dancing scarecrows on the path in front of Suzanne.

"What's going to happen to us?" Suzanne muttered, expecting no answer. An apathetic calm had embraced her; her feet seemed to drag her behind them.

"Who knows, Suzanne? We wait, we find out about these Aadae chicks, what their weak points are. That's all we can do. If we tried anything now, we got no chance. But we might later."

They reached the highway and stopped. Felice gestured at the domes across the road. "They live in those things, too," she said to Suzanne. "I found out yesterday. I looked inside one of their doorways. Exactly like ours."

Suzanne looked toward the city. She could barely see the tall rectangles and spires of its skyline. To the left of the city, the early morning sky was beginning to glow. Felice clutched her arm and she noticed the Aadae for the first time. They were sitting on the highway in a semicircle, soundlessly gazing east.

"Suzanne." She swung around and saw Gabe, his face almost white. His dark frizzy hair was a cloud around his head. "Are you all right? I followed you just to be sure; you didn't look too well."

"I'm fine. Where's Joel?"

"He fell asleep. Or passed out. I'm not sure which." Gabe looked apologetic.

She shrugged, then looked uncertainly at Felice. "Oh, Gabe, this is—"

"I know Felice, she was in my evening lit class." Gabe smiled. "She was the best student in it."

Felice was appearing uncharacteristically shy. She grinned and looked down at her feet. "Come on," she said. "You were a good teacher, that's all." Suzanne shuddered at the mention of the past. *She watched Joel as he slept beside her. His slim, muscled chest rose and fell with each breath. I love you anyway, Joel; there's been more good than bad. We just need time, that's all; you'll find yourself.*

Suddenly she hated the Aadae. She closed her fists, hoping for an Aada's neck around which to squeeze them. Tears stung her eyes, blurring the image of the Aadae in the road.

"What are they doing?" Gabe whispered. She ignored him and began to walk along the highway toward the aliens. A soft sigh rose from the semicircle of Aadae and drifted to her. They were swaying now, back and forth from the waist.

The sun's edge appeared on the horizon, lighting up the road. The Aadae leaned forward. Suzanne, hearing footsteps behind her, stepped forward and turned.

Five pairs of blind violet eyes stared through her. Startled, she moved away from the five Aadae and let them pass. The five, dressed in dirty robes, stumbled onto the road, arms stretched in front of them. They wandered to the edge of the semicircle and stood there, holding their arms out toward the sun. Suzanne followed them and stood with them. They didn't seem to realize she was there.

She waved an arm in front of the nearest Aada. The alien showed no reaction. *They're truly blind,* she thought as she gazed into the empty eyes. The five Aadae continued to stare directly into the rising sun. They began to sway on their feet, burned-out retinas unable to focus. She stepped back from them, moving again to the side of the road.

Gabe and Felice were with her, pulling at her arms. "Come on," said Gabe, "we'd better get out of here, come on." She pulled her arms free and continued to watch the Aadae.

Something was drawing her toward the aliens, something that hovered over her, tugging at her mind. She was at peace, wanting only to join the group on the road. She found her head turning to the sun.

A shadow rose in front of her. "Suzanne!" It was Gabe, holding her by the shoulders. Suddenly she was frightened. She stumbled backward, grabbing at Gabe's arms. The sighs of the Aadae were louder now, driving her away.

"Run!" Suzanne screamed. "Run!" Her feet, pounding along the side of the road, were carrying her back to the domes. She ran, soon losing herself among the domes. At last she stopped, exhausted, in front of one. She turned to the triangular doorway.

Two Aadae were there, one with stiff orange hair like a flame and shiny copper-colored skin. The dark-haired golden-skinned one was coming toward her. She threw up her arms, trying to ward her off.

The alien took her by the arm and tugged gently. Suzanne followed the Aada passively, led like a child along the path between the domes. Then they stopped and she realized that she was in front of her own dome.

She sighed and leaned against the doorway. Her fear had disappeared, and she was feeling a bit foolish. *I must have been really drunk.* The Aada released her, then bowed from the waist in an Oriental farewell before disappearing among the domes.

The air was heavy and the sky overcast. People were sitting or standing around aimlessly; occasionally small groups of people, scarcely speaking to each other, would pass by. Suzanne sat with her back to her dome, watching Felice mend a shirt. That morning, at breakfast, one of the men had stood up and thrown his bowl, still filled with greenish mush, at the wall. All of them had been growing tired of the food, which was always the same. But until today, they had simply gone to the slots on the wall, pushed the buttons, and passively accepted the green mush and milky blue liquid which were all the slots ever yielded besides glasses of water.

The green mush had stuck to the wall, resembling a fungoid growth. Rivulets ran from it, trickling to the floor. Then a tiny gray-haired woman hurled her bowl. Within seconds, everyone in the large room was throwing bowls and following the bowls with the glasses of blue liquid, shrieking with laughter as the liquid mingled with the mush on the walls. Several people hurried to the food slots and punched buttons wildly, pulled out more food and threw it at the walls. The orgy of food throwing had lasted almost half an hour until the walls were thickly coated and the Aadae had arrived.

The two aliens had ignored the mess. They brought a cart with them filled with oddly shaped metal objects of different sizes. One of the Aadae rummaged among the objects and removed a small cylinder. Then she held it over her head, showing it to everyone in the room. Her companion handed her a silvery block and the Aada attached it to the cylinder, then fastened a blue block to the cylinder's other end.

"Put together," the alien said, pointing with the object to the cart. The two Aadae turned and left the dome.

"What the hell," Suzanne heard Oscar mutter.

"We better do it," said the tiny old woman. "Who knows what they'll do if we don't."

The room was beginning to stink. A few flies buzzed near the mush-covered walls. "I'd better get Joel his breakfast," Suzanne said absently to Felice. She wandered over to the food slots, punched the buttons and removed a bowl and glass. People had already begun work on the objects by the time she was climbing the stairs to her room, where Joel still lay sleeping. *At least it's something to do.*

It had taken only a couple of hours to put the objects together. Once again, they were left with time on their hands, long hours that were chains on their minds, minutes through which they swam, pushed underwater, unable to come up for air. Felice was mending the shirt on her lap slowly and carefully; the sewing of each stitch became an entire project.

"They'll come back," said Suzanne. "And give us more pointless stuff to do."

"You know what I think," said the small woman. "I think they're crazy. They don't need us to put that stuff together." Felice hunched herself over the shirt and continued sewing. "You can't even tell what the things are *for*."

Suzanne began to poke at a loose thread on her jeans. The humid air was making her sweat and her crotch was starting to itch. She had managed to wash her underwear by using several glasses of water from the food slots, but there was nowhere she could bathe except by one of the sinks in the bathroom where the water was always cold and anyone could wander in at any time. Suzanne was afraid to go to the bathroom alone anyway. A woman in one of the nearby domes had been raped in a bathroom; although her husband had beaten the man who had done it, the fear of rape had spread among many women. Now Suzanne went to the bathroom only with Joel or Felice or some of the other women in the dome. A couple of times Gabe would accompany her, looking modestly away from her at the wall while she squatted on the floor over the hole which would suck her wastes away down a large tube. There were no partitions between the holes; squatting over them had become ritualized, with everyone courteously avoiding a look at the others present in the bathroom. Occasionally there was moisture around the holes; someone had taken a piss and missed. One fastidious young couple tried to keep the bathroom clean, mopping the floor and walls with an old undershirt, but they were not always successful.

Suzanne was growing uneasy. She was used to seeing an occasional pair of Aadae stroll along the pathway in front of her, but the aliens seemed to have disappeared. Suddenly her muscles tightened involuntarily. Something was in the air, hovering over her.

She heard a scream, a high-pitched, ululating sound, and then a roar, a bellowing from hundreds of throats. "Felice!" she cried, grabbing at the woman next to her. Felice dropped her shirt and they both stood up.

We should go inside. Suzanne looked down the pathway

and saw a large group of men moving toward the highway. She began to run toward them with Felice close behind her. Again she heard the scream, which had taken on the cadences of a mournful song. It was closer to her now. A small group of people had gathered in front of a dome up ahead. She ran to them and pushed her way through the crowd. Then she shrank back, moaning softly, slapping a hand over her mouth.

An Aada hung in the doorway by her feet. Someone had tied a rope around her ankles. The alien had been stabbed several times; brown clots covered her body. Her long orange hair brushed the ground as she turned in the doorway, her violet eyes stared sightlessly at the crowd. They were all that was left of her face, smashed by fists. Bone fragments protruded from her jaw; her copper-colored skin was covered by greenish bruises. On the ground beneath her lay another Aada, dying from wounds which covered her body. The alien on the ground drew her black hair over her chest, lifted her head slightly, and opened her mouth, and Suzanne again heard the song-like scream. Then she turned from them and was silent.

The people around Suzanne said nothing. She heard only their breathing, the sound of a giant bellows near a flame. She turned away from the alien bodies and stumbled back to Felice.

"We have to get out of here, Suzanne," she heard Felice whisper. Another roar reached her ears. She could see the crowd of men crossing the highway. Some of them had their arms raised. Knives glittered in their fists. An elongated shadow fell across the mob on the highway and she became conscious of a faint humming sound. An alien air vehicle was in the sky, a slender silver torpedo waiting to strike.

A bright light flashed across the highway soundlessly.

She threw an arm across her eyes and staggered backward. The people in front of the dome were running past her. An arm swung out and hit her, knocking her onto the path. She climbed to her feet, looking aimlessly around. The air vehicle was moving away to the north.

"Felice!" she cried out. Her voice shook. Then she saw that there were no longer any men on the highway, only burned, blackened bodies strewn about on the asphalt. The smell of charred flesh was carried to her nostrils and she bent over, vomiting quietly, arms wrapped around her shaking body.

"The fools." It was Felice's voice, harsh and bitter. "Too soon." A hand was on her shoulder, pulling at her gently. She looked over at Felice, then back at the highway.

A group of Aadae were there, looking down at the bodies. *Happy, aren't you? It wasn't even a contest.* There was no way now to tell who lay in the road, if anyone she knew was there. She would have to wait, find out who was missing, and that would take days. Any mourning would be general and unfocused. The Aadae began to circle around the bodies.

Then she heard the sobbing, deep and uncontrolled weeping. Three Aadae threw themselves down on the pavement, beating against it with their fists. The aliens were crying, not for the two Aadae who had been murdered, but for the men on the highway.

Felice was pulling her back along the pathway toward their own dome. As they retreated, Suzanne caught one last glimpse of the Aadae as they flung their arms open to the sun and heard once again their musical scream.

She heard Joel as he crept toward his mat in the darkness. She turned over and reached for him, brushing against his leg. He jumped back. "Jesus! Don't scare me like that."

"Joel, where have you been?"

"Where I was the night before."

"Where?"

"None of your goddamn business, Suzanne." He pulled off his clothes and sprawled on the mat next to hers.

"I just want to know, Joel."

"I can tell you're back to normal; you're going to revive the Inquisition. I'm tired. I'm going to sleep."

"You haven't gotten up one morning this week, Joel, ever since they started giving us that stuff to put together."

"I should care. You don't even know what the fuckers are *for*, you just sit there putting them together, you think it's really important, don't you, just like that dumb job at the warehouse you used to have."

"It's not that, Joel. They're going to find out you're not doing your share, and God knows what they'll do then."

"I could give a shit." She could hear him turn over on his mat and knew the conversation was finished. Suzanne had heard rumors about a group of men and a few women who would meet late at night to discuss what to do about the Aadae. She knew nothing more and was afraid to know even that much. She remembered the burned bodies on the highway and decided it was best simply to go about her business and wait.

She was pretty sure that Oscar Harrison was in the group and that Felice knew about it, although she doubted that the protective Oscar would allow his wife to go to the meetings. It wouldn't be hard for her to get involved if she wanted, but she preferred to wait and see if anything happened. She could act then.

"It's a perfectly good job, Joel; why are you always putting it

down?" She put down her beer and glared at him across the kitchen table.

"It's a dead end and you know it. That's all life is for you, getting by. You could do more and you know it, but it's easier this way—you don't have to think or try. It's even easier to put up with me; it's better than being alone. At least I know what I am; you don't even look at yourself."

I was practical, at least. Not that it mattered now. There had been no more money for her training in music, so she had left school and taken the job in the warehouse office, telling herself it was only temporary, she could still have her voice lessons, go to the local opera company's rehearsals at night. But she stopped going to the rehearsals—she was usually too tired—and then she had stopped going to the voice lessons. *I wouldn't have been much good anyway.* Occasionally she sang for her friends at parties, smiling when they told her she should become a professional; *it's just a hobby.* Then Gabe had rushed over one day to tell her that the opera was holding auditions, they needed a new soprano, she would be perfect, the pay wasn't much, but she could at least quit that office job. And she promised to go to the audition, but by then she was out of training, her voice roughened by cigarettes, so she didn't go after all. There was no point to it. She had just gotten a raise; no sense in throwing it away.

It doesn't matter. The Aadae were here and had no use for singers, nor for office workers. Her past was a meaningless memory, her possible future in that other world only a shadow of the wishes that had once crossed her mind. Better that she had had no great ambitions when the Aadae came; she would not have been able to stand it. Her dreams had already died.

It's just as well.

Shadows

* * * * *

The orange-haired alien was named Neir-let. Felice had mentioned that to her a couple of days before. Neir-let and her dark-haired companion were the Aadae who had instructed them in how to put together the metal objects which were now beginning to clutter the large downstairs room of the dome. Neir-let wore a blue gem on her forehead, a stone seemingly embedded in her skin, as did all the other Aadae. Suzanne hadn't even noticed this until Oscar had pointed it out; most of the aliens' foreheads were covered by their untidy hair. The gem was tiny, smaller than a Hindu's caste mark; it glittered, and Suzanne shivered involuntarily.

Neir-let had become more fluent in English, although no one could be sure about how she had learned it. Her companion never said anything. Neir-let had just demonstrated how to attach a silver globe to the apparatus they had been building, then she gave them a cartful of silver globes, several of which went rolling out of the cart over the floor, stopping their travels under the food slots. The metal objects on the floor were entwined in metallic tubing; the blocks and cylinders they had started out with were already hidden. The silver globes were to be attached to some of the loose ends of tubing.

Suzanne, sitting with Felice and a red-headed woman named Asenath Berry at one of the tables, reached for her bowl of mush. She was losing weight. Suzanne had already been thin before the Aadae came. On the diet of mush, she estimated, from the looseness of her clothing, that she had lost another ten pounds. A *scarecrow*. Her brown hair, always unruly, stood out around her head like a nimbus; there was no way to straighten it here.

No one made any move toward the objects they were

supposed to be putting together. They had all learned that Neir-let was fairly easy-going and didn't seem to care what they did as long as the work was completed by the evening. Neir-let was sitting on the floor near the doorway, picking what looked like small insects out of her hair. Her companion leaned against the wall, scratching her crotch.

Suddenly Oscar stood up and walked over to Neir-let. Suzanne glanced at Felice. The chatter in the large room died down. No one had dared to approach an alien directly up to now. Asenath Berry poked Suzanne in the ribs. "What the hell is he up to?" the redhead asked. Suzanne shrugged. Asenath had lost little weight on the mush diet; her round, braless breasts were an edifice under her sleeveless blue top and Suzanne wondered if Asenath had used silicone. Her long tanned legs were set off by her white shorts. How she kept them shaved was a mystery. Felice had said that Asenath was a prostitute, that she had come out of the city with a closetful of clothes and cosmetics carried by three of her most faithful customers. Asenath shared her room with a lean black man named Warren, who, like Joel, usually slept late. "A mack," Felice had told her, sneering at the word. *What do I care.* Suzanne had met Asenath one night in the hallway. The redhead had taken one look at her frail figure and pulled out two cans of beef stew hidden in her purse. "You need them more than me, honey." She had hurried back to her room to share them with Joel, who opened them with his knife, and they had eaten them slowly, relishing each bite. Since then, she found it difficult not to be friendly to Asenath, although at the same time she was a bit frightened of her.

"I just want to ask a question," Oscar said to Neir-let. The room was silent. Neir-let looked up at Oscar and smiled. "I just want to know what that blue thing in your head is."

The alien was still smiling. "Through it I am with those above," she replied, and shrugged as if that were self-explanatory.

"The others of your kind?" Oscar said slowly.

"No, except . . ." Neir-let paused. "I have no words." She smiled at Oscar and raised her hands, palms up. Oscar nodded and returned to Felice's side, looking thoughtful.

A few people got up and began to attach the globes to some of the metal objects strewn across the floor. "I think they still have spaceships overhead," Oscar said to Felice, "and she means they can contact them with those blue stones. That's all it could mean. At any sign of trouble, they could wipe us all out." He clenched his fists. Asenath was smiling at a burly man seated at the next table. Suzanne ate her mush, licking it off her fingers, forcing herself. Asenath stood up, motioned to the burly man, and left the room with him. The Aadae were paying no attention.

Somebody should do something. She finished the mush and looked around. Everyone was devoting full attention either to the breakfast mush or to the metal objects. Neir-let and her friend had moved outside and were staring up at the sky. Suzanne's arms seemed to freeze on the table near her empty bowl. She was unable to move, eyes fixed on her fingertips. Thoughts were chasing each other through her mind; she could grasp none of them. A heavy weight was pushing her against the table, preventing her from standing up and going to work on the metal devices.

Someone nudged her. "That ho's lookin' for you," Felice drawled contemptuously. She forced herself to look up and saw Asenath on the metal stairway, motioning to her. The burly man had disappeared. "Don't go," Felice went on. "You don't want to be with the likes of her." Then Oscar put a restraining hand on his wife's shoulder.

"Don't tell Suzanne what to do," he said quietly. "You go ahead," he said to Suzanne. She hesitated for a moment, then got up and walked to the stairway.

"Come on up," she called to Suzanne. She climbed the stairs.

"What is it?"

"I got two packs of cigarettes off my friend," Asenath whispered. She winked at Suzanne and her black eyelashes seemed to crawl over her eye like an insect. "Want a couple?"

"That was fast work," Suzanne said, trying to smile. Asenath's cold blue eyes showed no reaction.

"You better come to my room, or else everybody's going to want one." The redhead turned and Suzanne followed her past the first level of rooms and up the next flight of stairs. Asenath finally stopped in front of a doorway. "Come on in." Suzanne entered the room. Warren was sprawled across his mat, clothed in a pink shirt and velvety purple slacks. He held a small hand mirror and was fiddling with his moustache. "Have a seat," said Asenath, motioning to her mat. Suzanne sat, feeling uneasy.

Asenath didn't sit down. She peered out into the hallway, then strode over to Suzanne. "There aren't any cigarettes, kid, just some questions."

Suzanne opened her mouth. Her vocal chords locked and nothing emerged except a sharp gasp. She swallowed and pulled her legs closer to her chest.

"What's that man of yours been up to?" Asenath asked.

"I don't know," she managed to say. "I don't know what you mean." Her voice sounded weak, ineffectual.

"Stop being stupid. He's been out every night this week,

we know that, and we know where he is for some of the time. Now you tell us where he goes."

"I don't know."

"You're saying that a little too often; I don't want to hear it again. We've tried following him. We know he doesn't come back here right away. You must know something, he must have hinted at what he does."

Suzanne looked away from Asenath to Warren, who had put down his hand mirror and was staring blankly at the wall. "I don't know where he goes," she said, pronouncing the words carefully. "I don't know anything about his activities. Joel tells me nothing. He rarely told me anything, even before we all came here. Our relationship is not exactly what you would call open." She felt defeated and exposed before the red-headed woman and her dark silent partner.

"Christ," Asenath muttered.

"Let her go," said Warren. Suzanne stood up and began to move toward the door. A hand seized her shoulder and she found herself facing Asenath's blue eyes again.

"If you do find out anything," the prostitute whispered, "if he does decide to confide in you, you better let me know, I'm telling you, and right away. And you just keep quiet about this little talk."

She retreated from the room angry and frightened, afraid to stop now in her own room to wake up Joel. *I have to warn him. I have to find out. I have to talk to somebody.* She paused at the top of the stairway, apprehensive about joining the people in the large room below. But they were ignoring her, busy working on their alien devices.

She continued down the steps, avoiding a glance at Felice and Oscar. She sat down in a corner and began fitting metal pieces together under the casual, almost reassuring gaze of Neir-let.

★ ★ ★ ★ ★

"I have to talk to you, Gabe."

"Sure."

"Not here." Suzanne eyed the people sitting in front of Gabe's dome nervously and felt that they were all watching her. She forced herself to look at them directly and realized that they were paying her little attention. "I mean, I feel like walking around."

"Okay." Gabe hoisted himself off the ground and brushed off his dirty rumpled trousers. Oddly enough, he seemed to be maintaining his girth on the Aadaen diet. He took her arm gently. "Back to your room?"

"Joel's there. I mean, I think he's still asleep." She recognized a face in front of one of the domes and waved at it while nodding her head. "Let's walk on the highway."

The weather was warm but not humid. White clouds danced across the blue sky under the benevolent gaze of the sun. A group of adolescent boys had somehow gotten hold of a baseball and bat and were playing a game on the highway. Farther down the road, Suzanne could see a group of children with some Aadae. They too were playing a game, chasing what looked like cylinders on wheels across the safety islands. Suzanne and Gabe walked toward the city, past the baseball players.

"I have to talk about Joel," she said. "I'm worried."

"What's the problem this time?"

"It isn't just a personal thing, Gabe. I'm scared. Joel's been out nights, I don't know where he goes. Maybe it's none of my business, I guess I should be used to it by now. But the thing is . . ." She lowered her voice. "A couple of other people want to know where he goes, too, Gabe; they were asking me about it this morning. They weren't being gentle. I think they would have beaten it out of me if they thought I knew."

Gabe scratched at his beard. In the absence of razor blades he, like most of the men, was looking shaggier than usual. "You don't know where he goes?"

"For God's sake, Gabe. No, I don't. I thought you might. I thought you could tell me what's going on."

"I think you should tell me who wanted to know about Joel, Suzanne."

"Asenath Berry. You've seen her, the good-looking redhead, the whore. She and her friend Warren wanted to know. I was dumb enough to think Asenath wanted to be my friend."

Gabe sighed and was silent for a few seconds. She could hear the shouts of the baseball-playing boys in back of them. "I'll talk to her," Gabe said at last. "She won't bother you again."

"Then you do know something." She stopped walking and faced him. "Tell me. What is it?"

"I shouldn't tell you. I tried not to; I thought it was best that you stay out of it. But I guess you have a right to know. A group of us have been making some plans; that's all I can say. Joel's part of the group. So is Asenath. Some of us have been a little suspicious of Joel lately. It seems he doesn't go directly home from our little get-togethers. Asenath must have taken it upon herself to find out why."

She turned away from Gabe, bewildered. "Now I've just upset you," he muttered. "It's probably nothing. We're all a little paranoid; we have to be. We'll probably find out he's just visiting a friend or something. Don't worry, he's not that involved with us anyway; we've been holding meetings without him once in a while. I don't think he wants to get tangled up in anything too dangerous. You know Joel."

Gabe was leaving something out. Suddenly she didn't

want to hear any more, didn't want to know what Gabe or Joel or anyone else might be planning. "He's seeing someone else," she said. "He's seeing another girl. It's happened before." *That must be it.* The thought left her empty, almost relieved.

"Why do you stay with him, Suzanne?"

"I don't know. What difference does it make now?" She turned to the city. "Let's just keep walking, Gabe, let's go back to the city; they'll never find us there, we'll get Joel and go back and we can sit around drinking at Mojo's like we used to."

"You know we can't."

"Why not?"

"They'll find us. We should go back, Suzanne. Come on, I'll walk you to your dome."

"I'd rather not go back there right now," she said wearily. She went to the side of the road and sat down on some grass. "You can leave if you want, Gabe, I think I'd rather be alone right now anyway."

"You're sure, Suzanne? You'll be okay?"

"I'll be fine."

"You won't do anything silly?"

"No."

"Well, if you want to talk to me later or anything, feel free." She watched him shuffle back down the highway, shoulders slumped forward.

She pulled at the grass near her foot. Things were slipping away from her again as they always had. Her relationship with Joel had always seemed fortuitous. He had drifted into her life at a party she almost didn't attend; he could very well drift out again and there was nothing she could do about it. At worst he would get involved in some foolhardy scheme with Gabe and the others, resulting in disaster; she was convinced that the Aadae could not be defeated. At best, he would stay with her and they would continue living in the dome as they had with no purpose other than constructing alien objects for the Aadae. The thought made her shudder. It was useless to look ahead; the best thing to do was to get through each day, forfeiting any hopes. She had practice at that already.

A cloud danced in front of the sun, shadowing the road in front of her. She shivered in the cooler air.

Joel had disappeared again. In the morning, his mat was empty. Suzanne, awake at dawn, was outside the dome, shivering slightly in the wet air.

A heavy fog hung over the domed settlement, its gray masses almost indistinguishable from the metal domes. Its tendrils wound along the pathway and wrapped themselves around her feet. Suzanne stepped away from the doorway into the fog and was soon lost in its billowing masses, unable to see more than dim shapes. She was hidden and protected.

She was not looking for Joel. She didn't really want to know where he was and didn't want to risk confronting him in the presence of someone else. She tried to think about him objectively in the gray silence. It was foolish to think she could be everything to him, that she could fulfill all his needs, particularly in the present situation. He had always come back before. She demanded little sexually, content to satisfy Joel's needs with few of her own. She thought of Paul, whom she had loved while still in school. After two months, she had finally allowed Paul to share her cot in the dormitory room, twisting against him frantically during the night. She had satisfied him, but not herself. She avoided Paul after that. There was another, a boy whose name she couldn't remember, at a party, and with him there were only spasms and a drained, nauseous feeling afterward. With Joel she acted, going through the motions but always distant, her mind drifting off as he entered her. At times she would feel a twinge or an occasional spasm. She knew she loved him, or at least had loved him once; yet if he had remained with her, never touching her except for a kiss or a few hugs, she would have been content. *I can't expect him to be satisfied with that; no one would be. Why shouldn't he see someone else? It's surprising he stays with me at all.* Her heart twisted at the thought. Her mind throbbed, recoiling from the image of Joel with a vague female shape, and tears stung her eyes. She hated her body, a piece of perambulating dead meat, an anesthetized machine. *No, not anesthetized.* She could, after all, feel pain.

She was lost in the fog. She no longer knew where her own dome was. She kept walking, thinking that if she could find the highway, she could reorient herself.

"Hey." She turned. "Hey." Two young black men stood in the doorway of a dome, watching her. They were smiling, and one of them gestured to her. She fled into the fog, turning down another path and almost running until she was sure the two men were far behind. Then she suddenly felt shame. *They probably just wanted to ask me something.* She shook off the thought. *I have to be careful.* But she wondered if she would have hurried away if the men had been white. Her cheeks burned.

She was more lost than before. She stopped in front of a dome and tried to figure out where she was. She should have come to the highway by now.

She peered inside the dome tentatively, then stepped back. It was guarded by two Aadae. Inside, she could see aliens sleeping on the floor in the large central room. She had not seen the inside of one of their dwellings before, afraid of approaching one. The guards looked at her inquisitively. She backed away farther, trying to smile harmlessly, then continued on the path.

She collided with someone. She opened her mouth to apologize, then threw her hands in front of her face and managed to suppress a scream. A bald, wizened figure stood there, clad only in a dirty robe. It was no more than five feet tall and its greenish-yellow skin was stretched tightly over bones. It stared at her blankly and she recognized the violet eyes of the Aadae. Its robe hung open, revealing a penis no thicker than a finger. The blue stone on its forehead seemed to wink at her.

One of the males. She felt nauseated. The figure tried to reach for her, his lips drawing back across his teeth in an imitation of a smile. She moved back, trying to ward him off with her arms.

Then another Aada was beside him, holding his arm. She recognized Neir-let. The Aada was whispering to the male in her own language. The male, still grinning, sat down.

"He frightens you?" Neir-let asked. Suzanne sighed with relief. "He is harmless."

"I didn't know . . . I haven't seen a male Aada before."

Neir-let looked puzzled for a second, then nodded. "Male. We have few, enough for children. We always have few. This one is old and no longer wise." The male was drooling and picking at his toenails. "Soon his mind will join the others above. In his travels, he may see our home again." Neir-let sat down with the male, her arm across his shoulders.

"Do you miss your home?" Suzanne said impulsively. She was suddenly curious about the Aadae, who as far as she knew rarely talked to anyone. Neir-let seemed to sigh.

"To you, Suzanne, I will talk," said the alien. She was shocked, not realizing that Neir-let knew her name. "You have a gift, I know. You have brushed those above once in the dawn. Do you remember? You fled from us."

Suzanne struggled with her memories, then recalled the morning she had seen the Aadae seated on the highway, staring into the sun. She nodded silently.

"Yes, I miss my home. I will not see it again as I am. But I could not stay there knowing that other minds would die. Your world is much like ours, but the small differences bring me sadness. Yet I could live here with my daughters and be pleased." Neir-let paused. Suzanne sat down near her, for once unafraid. "But we must leave here and the home of my daughters must be the ship."

Leave here. If we wait long enough . . . "Why are you here?" she asked.

"So that you will not die."

"You've killed so many of us, though. Why?"

Tears glistened in the alien's eyes. "If we had not, others would have joined them. Then all of you would die. It is a painful thing, Suzanne." Neir-let patted the male alien on the head and trilled to him. He nestled against her. Suzanne was at peace, strangely, not wanting to leave Neir-let's side. The fog had lifted slightly. *I should get back to the dome,* she thought, unwilling to move.

From the corner of her eye, she saw a shape leave the doorway of the dome where the Aadae slept. She turned to face it. *Joel.* The shape disappeared in the fog and she could not be sure.

Neir-let was still singing to the male Aada. Suzanne rose and began to thread her way through the maze of paths. She could see more clearly now and soon managed to find her own dome.

She hurried inside and up the stairway. In her room, Joel lay on his mat, seemingly asleep. Yet his breathing was shallow and his hair and face were dotted with small beads of moisture. She wanted to speak to him, to question him. She clamped her lips shut and curled up on her own mat, nursing her pain and her fear.

She had to talk to Gabe. She had to tell him what Neirlet had said.

She went looking for him as soon as she was through with her work for the day. The bright sunlight had burned away the fog of that morning and by noon the weather was hot and humid. A group of people, among them Oscar Harrison and Asenath Berry, had gathered in front of the dome when she left, speaking to each other in low, angry tones. One man reached out and grabbed her as she passed and she tried to pull away.

"Let her go," said Oscar. The man released her. Suzanne retreated, then looked back. Everyone in the area seemed to be leaving the vicinity as if expecting trouble. Joel was still asleep upstairs and for a moment she wondered if she should go back and wake him up. *Better to let him sleep; he'll miss the trouble.* She went on to Gabe's dome.

Gabe was not in his room. One of his roommates, a frail-looking Chinese man named Soong, looked up as she entered.

"Do you know where Gabe is?" she asked him. "I have to talk to him." She felt impatient, on edge. "It's pretty important."

Mr. Soong smiled. "He is being entertained by a young lady, I believe, a few domes down. He has been away all night. You can find him there, but I do not know if he wishes to be disturbed."

The old windbag. "Which dome?"

"I am not sure. If you wish to wait here, you are welcome. Please be seated." The man nodded toward one of the mats which crowded the floor. "Gabe was indeed overwhelmed by good fortune. He was surprised when the young lady appeared last night and invited him to share her company. Usually he is back by morning, but she was a very attractive woman."

And he's always complaining about his lousy luck. "Thank you," said Suzanne, trying to be as dignified as Mr. Soong. "I'll come back later. Please tell him Suzanne's looking for him; he'll know who I am."

She went back out the door and down the stairway. She paused in the downstairs room, wondering if she should talk to Felice. Then she remembered the angry crowd in front of her dome. *I can't go back there.*

For the first time, it occurred to her that Neir-let might have spoken to her in confidence. Perhaps she didn't want Suzanne speaking to anyone else about their talk; maybe she would be angry if she found out she had. She shrugged off the idea. It couldn't hurt to tell someone and it might prevent them from acting rashly. She remembered the burned bodies on the highway. They could afford to wait, knowing that the Aadae planned to leave.

"Suzanne." Gabe was standing in the doorway. She hurried toward him. He was smiling contentedly. "I finally had some luck, this girl I hardly know . . ."

"Mr. Soong told me." She tried to smile back.

"Don't look so irritated. I'll start flattering myself by thinking you're jealous."

"Gabe, I have to talk to you. I was talking to one of the Aadae last night and she told me they were going to leave eventually, I don't know when, but that's what she said."

"Where did you see her?"

"I just happened to run into her, I was wandering around. Gabe, if we can just wait . . ."

"Suzanne, they won't leave until they've accomplished their purpose, whatever that is. It could be pretty hideous, you know."

"Neir-let said they want to keep us from dying."

Gabe wiped his forehead with the back of his hand. "No doubt she was speaking figuratively."

Someone outside was shouting. Suzanne shook her head and began to move toward the doorway. "What's going on," she said listlessly. Something seemed to be keeping her from looking outside.

Gabe was pulling at her hand. "Don't talk to Neir-let any more," he muttered. "In fact, I wouldn't advise talking to any of the Aadae unless you can't help it. Some people don't like it; you could get into trouble."

She was suddenly annoyed by Gabe. She withdrew her hand and went outside. A small group of people were standing in front of her dome. She wandered toward them. Something was in the doorway of the dome. She moved closer.

She saw Joel. A shock seemed to strike her body, paralyzing her. Blood rushed to her head and face. Her skin crawled over her stiff muscles, a cold piece of iron was resting in her belly.

Joel was hanging by his neck in the doorway. He had been stabbed several times. Someone had ripped off his shirt, revealing long scratches on his chest. His feet dangled loosely from his legs. Above him, someone had posted a sign: COLLABORATOR. His eyes were closed, the long lashes shadowing his cheekbones.

She began to push people aside as she walked to the

doorway. She stumbled near a knife carelessly abandoned under the slowly rotating body. She picked up the bloodstained weapon and began to hack at the rope that held Joel by the neck.

"Suzanne." Gabe was near her. His voice seemed to reach her ears from a distance. "Come away from here." She continued to cut the rope until the body fell at her feet, a flesh-covered sack of bones. One hand draped itself across her left ankle, then slipped away.

She stepped over the body into the large central room. No one was there. Unfinished metal devices were strewn across the floor. She heard footsteps clatter near her and turned around.

Asenath Berry crouched on the stairway. Her blue eyes were hidden behind dark glasses. The redhead had a large knapsack on her back. Suzanne moved toward her, still holding the knife.

"Wait!" shouted Asenath, holding up her arms. "He told us everything before he died—he admitted it—we made sure of that. He told them everything he knew about our group, about our plans. They promised him a reward." Asenath continued to creep down the stairs. "He was a traitor, do you understand? He was looking out for himself."

The redhead was only a few feet away from her. Suzanne lunged toward Asenath, knocking her on her side. She lifted the knife. Asenath's foot hit her hand, knocking the knife across the room. The redhead tried to climb to her feet. Suzanne grabbed the curly red hair and began to pull at it silently.

Hands clawed at Suzanne's legs. "Stop it!" Asenath was screaming. Holding the prostitute's head with one hand, she started to punch her in the breasts.

"For God's sake!" Gabe's big arms were around her, pulling her away from Asenath. She sagged against him, suddenly exhausted, staring at the clump of red hair in her left hand. Asenath got up and scrambled out the door.

Gabe was shaking her by the shoulders. She managed to get free and saw the knife against the wall near the stairway. She picked it up and tucked it under her belt. Then she walked outside.

The small crowd was still there. Ignoring them, she grabbed Joel's feet and began to drag him along the pathway behind her. The people moved away from her, receding until she could see no faces, only blurs. She dragged Joel past the gray domes until she reached the side of the highway. She collapsed next to him, one arm across his chest.

I should have been with you. She drew his head near her chest. *I should have helped you. I didn't even talk to you. I didn't even try to find out what was wrong.*

She waited, watching the body, thinking that he would start to breathe again, that he would speak and hold out his arms to her. *You once told me you were a survivor, you would live forever.* He would hold onto her and she would take him back to the dome and help him recover.

She waited. A few people hurried past her and on down the highway, toward the city. They were leaving, ready to make plans and take their chances away from the domed settlement.

She waited. Joel did not move, did not speak. She began to dig his grave in the dirt, scratching at the soil with her knife and hands. She continued to dig until her hands were bleeding and her shoulders were stiff and sore.

She looked up. The sun had drifted to the west. Joel was covered by evening shadows. Overhead, the silvery aircraft of the Aadae hummed past, heading for the city. She stood up, staggering a little, and watched them.

The towers of the city gleamed. Several aircraft were hovering over them, insects over a crown. The sudden flash of light almost blinded her. She stumbled backward, closing her eyes.

When she opened them, she saw only blackened ruins where the city had been. Then the charred hulks collapsed before her eyes and she saw only a burned-out pit. Nearby, she could hear the strange mourning cry of the Aadae.

She dropped to her knees and began once more to dig.

Suzanne lay in her room. Now and then, she heard footsteps pass the door. Bits of conversation would drift from the main room up the stairs to her. She lay on her mat, her arms and legs held down by invisible bonds. Occasionally she slept.

Time became waves washing over her gently. She floated, occasionally focusing her eyes on the ceiling. A dark shape with flaming hair leaned over her and she saw it was Neir-let. "We must finish our task," the alien whispered. "Please help." She closed her eyes and when she opened them again, the Aada had disappeared.

Joel was near. She could tell that he was trying to be silent so he wouldn't disturb her. He was rummaging in the kitchen, trying to cook the blueberry waffles he had surprised her with one Sunday morning. She turned on her side and saw Gabe sitting against the wall.

"I didn't know what they were going to do," he said. "It was a trick, that girl taking me to her room; they knew I was his friend; they didn't want me around." She opened her mouth, trying to speak. Her lips were cracked and dry. *Don't worry,* she wanted to say, *you can stay for breakfast;*

Joel doesn't mind. She closed her eyes and felt a wet cloth on her face.

When she woke up again, she was lying under a long coat. Someone had removed her clothes. "I washed you off," said Gabe. He was holding a glass of blue liquid. He lifted her head and helped her sip some of it.

"How long have I been here?" she managed to ask.

"Days. I thought you were going to die." He put her head back on the mat.

"No, I won't die." She looked at her arm on top of the coat. Her hands had become bony claws, the blue veins which covered her arm were a web. "I won't die," she said again, in despair.

"I'll stay with you if you want me," said Gabe. "I moved into the room next door, but if you want me here, I'll stay. Just tell me."

She shook her head, rolling it from side to side on the mat. "No."

"Think it over, at least." He patted her hand. She withdrew it from him slowly and placed it under the coat.

"No." She was floating now. The room grew darker and the walls seemed to shimmer. Again she felt a wet cloth on her face.

When she woke up once more, Gabe was gone.

Suzanne wandered through the large downstairs room and took a seat next to the wall. She gazed at the people sitting around the tables. The tiny gray-haired woman was absent. Warren, Asenath, Oscar, and Felice were gone, as were others she had known only by sight: a big red-haired fellow, a bony middle-aged blonde, an acne-scarred Puerto Rican. She remembered the burned city, and then Joel.

She picked up one of the metal devices near her. Three

cylinders, woven together with metallic tubing, were joined to three globes. The cylinders rested on golden rectangular bases. The whole apparatus was about three feet in height. She wondered absently if they would ever be finished. She put the device down and waited for the Aadae to arrive with more components.

She resumed watching the people at the tables. It was possible that some of them, even now, were planning a way to resist or defeat the aliens, but she doubted it. The city was still too vivid an example in their minds, most likely. Most of the resisters, the determined and forceful ones, had probably died there. *This crowd's like me,* she thought bitterly. *We'll get by.* She noticed that some of the people appeared uneasy and realized that she was glaring at them. She looked away.

Gabe's heavy denimed legs were in front of her. She waved him away, but he sat down in front of her anyway.

"You had any breakfast, Suzanne?"

"No."

"You should eat. If you want, I'll get you some."

"I ate last night; I don't want anything now." She didn't tell him she had vomited the meal in the bathroom, kneeling on the floor and holding her hair off her face with one hand. "Thanks anyway, Gabe," she said tonelessly. He seemed to expand visibly at that, as if taking her words as encouragement. He hovered over her like a beast of prey, his brown beard making her think of a grizzly bear. She hated him at that moment. *Always sniffing around; you wanted Joel to die, you son of a bitch.* She was quickly ashamed of herself. *He's just trying to help.* She grew conscious of the hairy legs concealed by her dungarees, and her halitosis; one of her teeth, with no dental care, was slowly, painfully, and aromatically rotting away. She almost chuckled at the thought of Gabe, or anyone else, desiring her sexually. She folded her arms across her breasts, *knobby little things,* and again thought of Joel and all the ways in which she had failed him. Yet part of her still knew that regret was her justification, enjoyable for those who were seasoned to it, a way of believing that things could have been different. *Give me a thousand chances, and I would be the same.* That thought too had its comforting aspects. Her mind curled up inside her and continued its self-flagellation with the willows of guilt, leaving its peculiarly painful and pleasurable scars.

Gabe jostled her elbow. Neir-let and her companion were at the doorway, but this time they brought no components, only two small leatherlike pouches. Neir-let surveyed the room, apparently waiting for everyone's full attention; then she began to speak in her musical voice.

"We have almost finished assembly of these tools," she said. Suzanne straightened her back at the words. "Only one thing remains." The alien leaned over and picked up one of the metal objects. "Each of you should select one now, and keep it with you at all times." Suzanne reached over for the one she had handled before and watched as everyone scrambled about. No one appeared angry or relieved; they clutched the objects passively and silently, then retreated to the walls, seating themselves on the floor.

Neir-let opened her pouch and took out a small blue gem. It winked in the light and was seemingly answered by the blue stone embedded in Neir-let's forehead. "You will place this in the small dent you will find in one of the globes. It will adhere to the surface by itself." Neir-let and the other Aada began to move around the room, handing a blue stone to each person. Suzanne accepted hers from Neir-let and soon found the dented globe. She pressed the stone into the dent and waited.

The task was completed by everyone in a few minutes. Neir-let walked back to the doorway and held up her arms. "What I tell you now will be the hardest thing to do," she said. "You must sit with these tools and wait, concentrating on them as much as you are able. You may go outside if you wish, or sit by the road. If you grow weary, rest, then try again."

The two Aadae left the dome. Suzanne got up and began to follow them with her device. Gabe caught her by the arm.

"Where are you going?"

"Outside to concentrate," she replied. "What else can I do?"

"Don't. I wouldn't be surprised if they were trying to turn us into a group of zombies. Forget it. Let them try to force us; there's no way you can compel a person to concentrate."

She pulled away from him and went outside. She didn't care about the device. She wanted to get away from Gabe and the dome, sit alone with her thoughts. She walked toward the highway and seated herself next to the mound under which Joel lay. She would keep her vigil with him.

She put the metal object down at her side and found herself distracted by the blue gem. It seemed to tug at her mind, drawing her attention to itself. She continued to stare at the stone, secure in its blue gaze. Her mind was steady, hovering over her body, able to look at the grave near her with no sadness. She was at peace.

Somehow she managed to withdraw from the object. She rose unsteadily to her feet. It was almost noon. Her feet were asleep, her back stiff. She stomped around, trying to restore her circulation.

"Suzanne." Neir-let was standing by the mound. "You have seen?"

"What is this thing? What does it do, Neir-let?" It was the first time she had addressed the Aada by name and her tongue slid uncertainly over the words.

"It is a tool to build strength. It will aid you, but in a short time you will not need it, I think."

Suzanne turned from the alien, and noticed that a group of boys were playing baseball on the highway, while others sat on the side of the road in conversation. She saw only one woman, outside a dome, concentrating on her device. "No one else seems to be bothering."

"It does not matter," Neir-let said. "One, or a few, will lead and they must follow. You will see. A few are more receptive."

Suzanne sat down again, with her back to the device. "You will see," Neir-let's voice whispered.

Suzanne continued to concentrate, sometimes in the evenings, sometimes in the early mornings before the others were awake. Her days consisted of long periods in front of the device, punctuated only by the need to return to the dome for sleep and, less often, food.

Gabe came to her once, as she sat by the highway. He carried her and her device back to the dome and insisted upon forcing food down her throat. He hid the device in his room, saying he would give it back when she looked healthier. Suzanne shrugged at this, by now indifferent to her bony limbs and slightly swollen belly. She wondered vaguely if she was pregnant; her period had not yet arrived. She spent several days lying on her mat, passively bearing Gabe's ministrations and wondering what Joel's child would be like. But after a week, her womb bled once more and she knew that there was now nothing left of Joel except the decaying body under a mound.

She regained her strength and managed to steal her device from Gabe's room while he slept. She fled from her dome and resumed her vigil farther up the highway. She ate her meals in another dome and slept in its large main room, arms draped over the metal object.

She often began her meditations while a group of Aadae sat in the road greeting the dawn. Her mind became clearer, more conscious of the things around her. She focused on a series of sharp images: the shadows of the seated, swaying Aadae, slender and elongated, rippling along the bumps and crevices of the pavement—

the blinded eyes of the robed aliens, violet irises afloat on a sea of white, with pupils that became small dark tunnels into darkness—

a strand of blue-black hair on a golden cheek, caressed by the invisible fingers of a breeze, becoming a long moustache over a lip—

a blade of grass among its fellows, its roots deep in the ground, attempting to draw moisture from the dandelion that hovered over it menacingly.

Her mind uncoiled and floated above her, drifting over the seated Aadae. The domes beneath her grew smaller, becoming overturned bowls on a table and then the tops of mushrooms. She was soaring over the burned bones of the city, strewn in a black pit, an omen to be read by a giant seer. She felt no fear as her mind traveled over the Earth and did not attempt to draw it back. She circled over the city. The highways were asphalt runes, incomplete, leading only to the pit.

Her mind came closer to the ground and returned to her, rushing through the domes where people still slept, dolls thrown on the mats by a careless child. She was staring once again at the metal apparatus in front of her.

Almost ready. It was a whisper, in her mind but not of it. The Aadae rose and began to walk back to their dome, leading their blinded sisters by the hand. Suzanne blinked. There were black spots before her eyes and she realized that she must have been staring at the sun for part of the time.

Her body was a burden which she hoisted to its feet. She would rest, and feed herself, then let her mind roam again.

An Aada near her began to wail. Suzanne opened her mouth and sang with her; her soprano was a bird flying over, then alighting on, the alien's clear mellow contralto. She soared effortlessly, and her crystalline tones circled over the lower voice, then flew on over the clouds to the sun.

Suzanne sat by the highway, away from the late afternoon shadows cast on the ground by the domes. She set her device in front of her and prepared her mind for its work.

She was suddenly frightened, and remembered the morning, long ago, when she had fled from the Aadae in fear. *Throw it away.* She recoiled from the metal construct before her. *Someone, please, tell me what to do.* The world was silent, the road empty.

Once more. She watched the blue stone on the device. It began to grow larger, drawing her mind into a blue vortex. She swam in a shimmering dark sea and shafts of light, sharp as spears of glass, pierced her eyes.

She was hurtling over the Earth, following the sun to the west. She moved through the eye of a storm and danced on the pinwheel of clouds. The Earth shrank beneath her and she turned to the moon, brushing against its rocky lifeless surface. Its craters were empty, its mountain peaks sharp, its shadows cold. She fled from the moon and was lost in darkness, heavy black velvet draped over her, pressing at her.

She pushed the blackness away. Now she was falling, spiraling uncontrollably toward the sun. Its flaming surface was a battleground screaming across space, crying for death, reaching out to immolate her. Two flares erupted on the surface and became wispy appendages, the arms of a lover seeking an embrace. *No.* The star thundered at her. Another flare rose and flung her into the emptiness.

A whisper reached her, almost as insubstantial as the flare dissolving around her. *Not yet, you are not ready.* Frightened, she flew from the conflagration, moving outward until the planets were round pebbles and the sun only a distant lantern.

An invisible web surrounded her, pulling her toward a far red ruby glittering among diamonds. She passed a young world, still boiling, streaked with red and yellow streams. The red star in front of her grew larger and she drifted through its diffuse strands, to be met on the other side by a shaft of blue-white light. A tiny white sun circled the red star, a fierce sentry ready to defend its tired companion. She was pulled on, past a large gaseous world where heavy tentacled beasts fought in green seas, past a blue star around which dead rocks revolved, past a yellow sun linking flare-arms with its twin. She struggled against the web around her. *Take me back.* The web traveled more rapidly and she could catch only a glimpse of the worlds she passed.

Ahead of her lay clusters of suns, crowded together in the galactic hub, revolving slowly with companions or shrieking in death, murdering servant worlds around them. She whirled over them and retreated into memory:

Herds of automobiles stampeded through the streets. Their motors were an omnipresent growl, a subliminal threat. Trucks, oblivious to the smaller beasts around them, rolled by majestically; smaller cars made up for their lack in size by the use of clever tactics and, occasionally, increased belligerence. Suzanne walked the streets on a summer evening, clinging to Joel. She gazed up at his face and his eyes were momentarily two suns winking at her. She jostled a red-nosed drunk, rubbed elbows fleetingly with a young blonde woman whose cold green eyes became a green gas giant surrounded by rings. Ahead, a well-dressed silver-haired man shimmered, brushing aside luminous wisps before disappearing into a bar. Two adolescent girls flirted with three muscular boys dressed in embroidered denim jackets twinkling with constellations. She sniffed at the summer air: acrid odor of sweat, exhaust fumes, a whiff of aftershave, a charcoal-broiled steak, sulfur, ammonia, dust. Voices shrieked, babbled, murmured, roared, giggled, and bellowed, underscored by the insistent rumbling of the vehicles around them. She and the others began to retreat from the sidewalks, yielding them to the night. From her window, she could see the lighted windows in the towers around her. A dog was baying below. She heard a thunderous roar, then saw light on the street beneath her. Men on motorcycles screamed by, night creatures in search of prey.

A comet streaked past, throwing her from the starry city. She whirled through the tendrils of a nebula, spinning aimlessly into space. The intangible web which had held her disappeared. She was alone. She had no tears to cry for Joel, for her lost city, for the Earth now impossibly distant from her. She spun through the darkness, away from the pinwheels and discs of galaxies.

Something nearby was tugging at her mind. She drifted toward it, unable to resist. She did not belong here with her small fearful mind and her passive ineptitude. She could not deal with anything out here; she could not understand the processes that produced this immense spectacle, nor could she deal with it emotionally except as a series of frightening visions. Her mind seemed to contract, pushing in upon itself. *You are less than nothing here.*

Stellar corpses. She could not see them, but she felt their presence. Heavy chains dragged at her, drawing her on. She was a prisoner and assented to her bonds passively. It seemed somehow right that she should remain here, punished for having ventured too far.

Ahead, she saw a circle of blackness, darker even than the space around her, a deep well blotting out the nearer galaxies.

She was falling, tumbling forward into an endless pit. The black well grew wider. She cried out soundlessly and tried to crawl away with nonexistent limbs. *But I should wake up now.* The well surrounded her and she continued to fall.

The web was around her once more. *Pull away.* She tried to grasp the mind near her. The black pit was luring her on, teasing her with strands of light, whispering promises. *Resist.* The other mind touched her and she clung to it, struggling away from the hole in space.

Help me, she called to the other.

Help yourself. She pushed and the hole became a distant blot, then faded from sight. Streaks of blue and red light raced past her and she was ripped into a thousand pieces, beads on the thread of time. A thousand cries echoed in the vault of space and became one scream.

She was in the web, hovering over the Earth. She flew

closer and rested above a pink cloud over her domed settlement. It was already morning below and she could see tiny specks huddled together on the highway.

You will grow stronger, the other mind whispered to her. *You will travel with the other minds of space, streaking among the stars with tachyonic beings who have transformed their physical shapes ages ago. You will meet those who abandoned their bodies but lurk near their worlds, afraid to venture further. And if you are very strong, you may approach a star where the strongest dwell, ready to fight you if you intrude. They will try to fling you far away, but if you contend with them long enough, they will reveal their secrets and allow you to join them. Your mind will grow stronger with each journey, and when your body can no longer hold it, you will leave it behind, a garment which you have outgrown, and journey among the stars. You will learn all one can learn here and then move on to where there is only unending reflection. Do you understand?*

Yes. She was sitting by the highway once again, held by the receptacle of her body. Neir-let was with her, clasping her hand.

"There is one more thing to do," the Aada murmured. "Are you strong enough, or must you rest?"

"Now," said Suzanne. Her mind floated up, brushed against Neir-let's, then leapt from her across the Earth. She was a spark, a burst of lightning striking every human brain she found, leaping from one to the next. She seized a group of minds and flung them away, watching them leap to other minds. Then she gathered them all to her and wove them into her net, four billion strands, and flung them from the Earth. They cried out to her, some in fear, others in awe, still others in delight. She drew them back and wound the fabric around her, caressing each thread.

She was once more at Neir-let's side. Exhausted, she

rested her head on the Aada's shoulder. Neir-let's hand brushed her hair gently. Trapped in her body, Suzanne could still feel the bonds that linked her mind with all of humanity, and knew that they were now linked for all time. They would never be alone again, isolated and apart, shadows lingering in separate caves. However distant they might be, in thought or space, whatever they might do by themselves, they would all be joined as closely as lovers.

Neir-let stood up and removed the blue stone from the metal device. "You no longer need this," she said, gesturing at the apparatus. The Aada pulled a pointed knife from the belt over her briefs, reached over and pricked Suzanne's forehead, then pressed the stone against it. Suzanne bore the slight pain silently, wincing a bit, becoming calm as the stone pulsed between her temples. "This will help you to focus your mind, but soon you will not need it either."

Suzanne lifted her hand to her head, touching the stone. Other aliens nearby were already at work, embedding the small stones in the foreheads of people seated by the road. She stood up. A group of boys, stones glittering on their brows, approached her, palms open in thankfulness. She reached out to them with her mind and embraced them, crying out silently in joy.

Suzanne, clothed only in a tattered robe, stood in the doorway of a dome. The Aadae would teach humanity all that they knew before leaving for another world. Then mankind would have to ready its own ships and prepare to save another race from the oblivion of death. She knew her body would not last long enough to undertake the journey, but she would be with the ships, helping them to locate beings that still huddled together in fear.

She looked around her. The body of Gabe Cardozo was

nearby, propped up against a wall, face empty of expression. Rivulets of saliva ran down his beard and she smiled, knowing that his mind was out among the stars. Other people sat in small groups with Aadae, trying to learn what was necessary for their future voyage.

She had done her share, and knew no more would be asked of her. She left the dome and walked to the highway, wanting only to roam through space again. She joined the group of Aadae seated in the road, blind eyes staring upward. A naked child ran past her, heedless of the festering sores on his arms and belly.

She sat down next to the Aadae and lifted her eyes to the flaming disc overhead. Her mind floated up effortlessly, drifting through the clouds.

The turbulent yellow star ahead seemed to beckon her. *I'll be ready for you, I'll take your wisdom with me before you fling me away.* She unfurled her wings and flew toward the sun.

Behind the Eyes of Dreamers

Orielna's courage nearly failed her as she left her flyer and approached the gate. The north-south wall hid the rising sun, its wide shadow a dark band at her left and right. The short, tended grass of the plain was weedier near the base of the wall; a gnarled, thorny bush grew next to the gate.

She shivered. Beyond the wall was the Garden, with its tangled vines, unpruned plants, and towering trees. Unchanged people lived there, creatures without links who still endured aging and death and met their end long before their minds were completely clogged by memories. Calling this place the Garden had been a joke of some kind, a reference to a mythological garden where the first human beings had lived. The unchanged ones who lived here now were innocent of knowledge and untouched by sin.

All except one, Orielna reminded herself. The man she sought had come here to hide from the consequences of his deed.

A lens winked in the smooth metal surface near the gate. When Orielna had been scanned, the door slid open; she entered, already longing to retreat, and tried to ignore the whisper of the door as it closed behind her. The forest was green with light, and the air felt wet and heavy; she had not expected the Garden to be so shadowed.

"So she sent you," a voice said. "She wouldn't come herself."

Orielna looked around, startled, then saw the woman standing under a nearby tree. The link embedded in her forehead could have alerted her to the woman's presence, but Orielna was afraid to open its channels now. The woman's long pale hair was an unruly mass, and her brown shirt was torn; her violet eyes darted restlessly. Orielna shuddered as she remembered the message this woman had sent, insisting that Orielna and Aniya link with her and experience Josef's assault.

"Kitte," Orielna said softly, "I didn't expect to find you here."

"Aniya should have come herself. She's responsible for him—she's his sharer."

"So am I."

Kitte's mouth twisted. "You're only Aniya's eidolon. You and Josef are no more than reflections of her thoughts. She sent her shadow to find him."

Orielna tried to pity Kitte, but could not. The woman might have chosen to forget Josef. He was no longer a threat to her; alone and lost in the Garden, he might already be suffering for his act. But Kitte wanted him punished and had the right to demand that. Aniya had imprinted Josef with her thoughts and was therefore responsible for his deeds; she had to see that they were not repeated.

"I'll find him," Orielna said, folding her arms to conceal her trembling hands. "Aniya's my sharer, so it hardly matters which one of us conducts the search, since I know Josef's thoughts as well as she does. You'll have what you want when he's found."

"If you find him."

"I'll have help. A man here has offered to guide me." She stepped forward; Kitte was still blocking the only path through the underbrush. "Please let me pass."

"I know why Aniya didn't come. He was trying to escape her when he came to me—she can't bear the thought of facing him and seeing that trapped, frightened look in his eyes. She's afraid he might do to her what he did to me."

"He would have done nothing," Orielna said, "if you'd let him go. You shouldn't have tried to keep him." Her emotions were racing; she knew that she should open her link and bring herself into balance.

Kitte said, "He killed me. You don't know what it's like, feeling your life rushing from you, then being alive and knowing you were dead, that the break in you will never heal."

"But I do know," Orielna said. "You insisted that we link with you, after all." She did not want to remember how Kitte had flooded her mind with her memories during the link, how Josef's hands had closed around the woman's throat. He had been smiling; his large dark eyes had gleamed with joy. "But you didn't leave him much of a choice. Instead of letting him go, you ordered your helpmind to keep him locked inside your dwelling—he couldn't escape without breaking your will. He couldn't have meant to kill you. He only wanted you to release him." Even as she said this, she knew it wasn't so. Josef might have been only fearful at first, desperate to get away, but he had meant for Kitte to die as soon as his hands found her throat.

"He could have been happy with me," Kitte said. "He was so unhappy when I found him in the Garden. I would have done anything for him, you know." The woman's intensity and disordered emotions repelled Orielna; Kitte was wallowing in longing and rage. "He'll pay for it when you bring him out. He'll pay for murdering me."

I can leave now, Orielna thought, walk out of this Garden, return to Aniya, and leave the pursuit of Josef to others. She dismissed the notion; she could not abandon him now. If she brought him back to Aniya, he would be safe, however unhappy he was at being with the sharer he had wanted to escape; he could live as long as he never left Aniya's side. If Aniya surrendered responsibility for her eidolon, others would hunt him; he would surely endure erasure then and might even be destroyed. Kitte might demand the right to decide his fate herself, since she had been his victim. Perhaps Josef would prefer the loss of his thoughts and memories or even the destruction of his body to imprisonment with Aniya.

They would all suffer, whatever happened to Josef. Aniya would struggle to bend him to her will or else endure the pain of having him wiped; she would wonder how the man whose thoughts reflected her own had grown to hate her. She would have to imprison him in her house as long as he remained as he was so that others would be safe from him. Orielna would be trapped with both of them, feeling their pain inside herself whenever she reached out to them.

Kitte, of course, wanted them all to suffer. She would probably take as much joy in that as Josef had in murdering her.

"Let me give you some advice," Orielna said. "Drop the memory of your death. You'll just find it harder to remain in balance if you don't."

"Oh, no. I want it. I won't go through that little death to lose the memory of the one he brought to me. I won't let him have that victory—I won't give up part of myself, not yet, not until he's paid for what he did. I want to feel that fully."

Orielna edged past Kitte, ready to shove her aside if necessary, but the other woman moved out of her way. "You want to strike at me, don't you?" Kitte shouted after her. "The same thoughts were put into your mind and his, so you must feel the way he would. You can't even have your own feelings, eidolon!"

Orielna hastened into the forest. Kitte pitied her, and there was no reason for pity. She asked nothing more than to be her sharer's eidolon and to reflect Aniya's thoughts; she had not wanted to leave Aniya to come here.

No, she thought; that wasn't quite true. Though Orielna had at first wanted to go, to be apart from Aniya for a while, she had later begged Aniya not to send her on this search because she feared what it might do to her. She might diverge and become whatever Josef was now.

An eidolon—Kitte had lashed her with the word, as if it were an insult. The term was somewhat misleading. An eidolon's body did not have to resemble that of its creator; its mind was the eidolon cast in another's image. Aniya, alone in her house, shunning other people, had wanted a companion, someone with whom she would always be in perfect accord. The Net of minds, the interlinked intelligences that served everyone, had only to draw on its store of human genetic material to mold a body to Aniya's specifications, then bring it rapidly to maturity before impressing the pattern of Aniya's mind on the new being. Josef had been Aniya's first eidolon, Orielna the second. Josef had his sharer's dark hair, while Orielna was blond, but their eyes were Aniya's large black ones. All their memories, thoughts, and feelings were Aniya's; their sharer could look into their eyes and see herself.

They should have been content in Aniya's house, reflecting their creator's thoughts, their solitude undisturbed by contact with the presence of others. Once, they had been in perfect accord, passing their days in the games and simulated experiences Aniya preferred. Aniya's helpmind, the nexus that expressed itself through their dwelling, had been imprinted with her thought patterns and knew their desires so well that they rarely had to address it directly as it saw to their needs. Their peaceful days were untroubled; Aniya's happiness was their own.

Yet Josef had left them, and Aniya had been too distraught to stop him. Orielna recalled the cruel words he had spoken before he closed his link and descended the hill outside the house, determined to find out what he was apart from Aniya; he could no longer endure the sight of her. He had taunted her with that, mocking the way she had tried to fill her little world with other versions of herself.

"You love yourself," he had said. "You can't bear the presence of anyone else. But there must be some self-hatred inside you, too, or I couldn't want to leave you so much. You've wiped every memory of yours that might cause you pain, which means there are things inside you that you can't face, and I'm forced to share your uncertainty about what you are—what I am. I won't erase anything, though—I want to remember what I'm leaving behind. I want to see every part of you that's in me die while I become something more than your reflection."

Days had passed before Aniya recovered, and Orielna had felt as abandoned as her sharer did. They had finally convinced themselves that he would return. He was too much like Aniya; he could not live among other people. They had smiled a little over his absurd notion that he could, as he put it, become what he might have been. He would have been nothing without Aniya; he lived only because she had requested him from the Net. He had been only a lifeless body, a blank slate, a mass of biological material shaped to suit Aniya's tastes, awaiting the imprint of her thought patterns. He was hers; when he realized that, he would come back.

But he had not returned, and then Kitte's message had arrived. Why had he killed her? He would have known that her link was open, that she would be restored to life, demanding that Aniya take responsibility for her eidolon. He must have thought his violent deed would compel Aniya to have him erased; that was one sure way of escaping her for good.

Orielna was like Josef; she knew that she should be able to sense his motives. He could never have killed Kitte if his link had been open; the minds would have kept him in balance. He probably regretted it now; he might even be hoping that he would be found and restored to his sharer. That thought cheered her for only a moment. Away from her and Aniya, Josef might have diverged; he might have changed too much for them ever to see their thoughts mirrored in him again. If that was so, having him erased might be a mercy for all of them.

She halted and leaned against a tree. She had strayed from the path and could no longer see the wall through the forest. She opened her link so that it could guide her to her destination, a hut some distance away where a hunter named Daro lived. Josef was in the Garden somewhere, his link closed so that no one could track him that way, alone, perhaps desperately afraid. He might be ready to leave by the time she found him.

She thrashed her way through the thick foliage, prodded gently by her link in the right direction whenever she strayed. This place shouldn't, she thought, be called the Garden; gardens were tamed, planned to delight the eye and bring peace to the mind. Daro might have led her through this unruly growth, but had insisted that she make her way to his hut by herself. She had been told to bring no more than a wand and a pack of supplies. Beads of sweat dotted her forehead; she longed for the cooler, dryer air of Aniya's house, for all the comforts and aids that were forbidden here.

She considered what she knew about Daro. The man was connected to the world outside the Garden only by his link. He came to the wall for supplies, but had not passed through the gate to the other side for many years. He occasionally acted as a guide to those wishing to explore the Garden, and he had agreed to help her. He lived alone. His past before he had entered the Garden was, at his command, locked away in the records of the Net and was inaccessible to anyone else, but that was not uncommon. Aniya had closed off her own past life before fading her memories. Perhaps Daro had also chosen forgetfulness.

Orielna opened her link fully, hoping to find a message from Daro. He had to know that she was in the Garden. She heard nothing, then closed all the channels except the one linking her to the Net. She did not even know what the hunter looked like; his image was something else he chose to hide.

It did not matter. Daro would help her, for she could never find Josef by herself as long as his link was closed. She dampened her thoughts and trudged on.

She was still far from Daro's home when the night grew too dark to see. Her link could have guided her through the darkness, but the long walk had wearied her. She climbed up a small hill and sat down under the trees, keeping her wand and a small globe of light at her side. The light would keep animals away, but she was prepared to stun any that approached.

The leafy branches overhead hid the night sky. She missed the familiar sight; with Aniya, she had often sat in their courtyard, gazing at the stars and the specks of light that marked the Hoop of Habitats.

Most of humanity lived in the hollowed-out asteroids and glittering metallic eggs of the Hoop that encircled the Earth, shaping their worldlets to please themselves. In the past, other Habitats had fled the solar system, scattering like seeds into deep space. The people in the Habitats that remained felt no need to wander, finding enough unknown territory in their own minds, wills, dreams, and desires.

Long ago, human beings had created the Net of cybernetic mentalities to serve them. They had seeded near-space with their Habitats and had transformed the barren, hellish, sister-planet of Venus into a world of tropical gardens, tree-covered mountains, and warm, wide oceans. They had set a bracelet of Habitats around Mars and had made Earth's moon burgeon with life. They had banished the deserts creeping across Earth's lands and then, as though exhausted by their labors, they found rest in their Habitats and on the garden worlds they had created.

Once, according to the Net of minds, the planet-dwellers and those who lived in the Habitats had been separated by suspicion and distrust, but their links with the Net had drawn them together in the end. Those who had sought to transcend the bounds of human nature were now wandering the cosmos. The descendants of those who had rejected the linking of humankind with the Net hid in Earth's Garden and in the wilder lands of Venus and the Moon.

The rest lived in the dream their ancestors had imagined. Orielna, like her sharer, was moved whenever she contemplated the efforts of those who had made her peaceful life possible and who had not lived to experience their dream. Lately, however, thinking of the past made her feel mournful and adrift, and she had no right to be unhappy.

Any misery was an affront to those long-dead dreamers. She wondered why the Net allowed unhappiness to exist.

A creature hooted overhead; something howled in the distance. "Daro?" she called through her link. No one answered.

The night amplified her loneliness and fear. She wanted to reach out to Aniya through her link, but her sharer had not wished to experience this search with her. Orielna had understood why immediately. Aniya did not want to endure the difficulties and uncertainties of the search until it was over and Josef was restored to her.

She stretched out, keeping her wand under her hand. Her link was open; if harm came to her here, the link would call upon all of her body's resources to heal her and would summon aid. She tried to console herself with that fact, yet knew she could die in the Garden.

She had rarely thought about death before Kitte's message. She might die, but as long as her link was open, she could be revived. Any damage to her body would be repaired. If any of her memories were lost in the moment of death, the Net would restore them; she would not even know they had been temporarily lost.

Knowing this did not comfort her now. Against all reason, she found herself wondering if death were a kind of erasure, if it was the once-dead person who lived again or only a resurrected body with a duplicated mental pattern replaced by the minds. Such a person would be like an eidolon, but one unaware of what it was. It would heal and have its memories, but would it be the same person?

This idea was too disturbing to entertain for long, but others must have thought it. Maybe the minds of the Net knew it to be true and kept the knowledge from humanity, as they protected people from so much else. Perhaps this was why they insisted on punishing or restraining any murderer, even though the dead could be revived. Josef might be a murderer in the truest sense; Kitte had claimed that the break inside her would never heal. Her earlier self, now lost, had no one else to speak for it.

Aniya doesn't care if I die, Orielna thought. She hasn't come here because she's guessed how final death can be; she knows that if she died, only her eidolon would live afterward. But I'm only an eidolon now. It doesn't matter what happens to me; she'd never know the difference, and neither would I.

Maybe I don't want to be hers anymore.

The notion shocked her. She quickly brought herself into balance and closed off her thoughts before falling asleep.

The forest was filled with the songs of birds. Orielna waited until the patch of sky above was lighter, then went down the hill toward a creek. She did not have much farther to go; this stream would lead her to Daro's home.

The Garden was still strange to her. Aniya had no plants in her tiled courtyard, and the land around her house and hill was flat and open to the sky. Here, Orielna felt as if the trees might close in around her. How had Josef dared to come here with his link shut and no one to help him? She composed herself and began to follow the narrow waterway.

She walked for most of the morning in a subdued trance before her link alerted her that Daro was near. As she rounded a bend in the creek, she saw a clearing just above the rocky bank. A man holding a wand was waiting outside a hut.

"Daro," a voice whispered through her link. Orielna approached him cautiously, then raised a hand to her lips in dismay. The hut behind him was a primitive structure of wood and grass, and Daro didn't look like any of the images of people she had seen. He was a small, muscular man with ungroomed curly brown hair and sun-browned skin, his only clothing stained white shorts and muddy sandals. Could the minds have chosen to create such a man, or had someone with a distorted aesthetic sense selected his qualities? His body seemed too thick, his muscles too sharply defined.

"Took you long enough to get here," he said, his voice low and harsh. "But I was wondering if you'd get here at all."

She swallowed. "I was hoping you'd find me and lead me here yourself."

Daro shrugged. "Some people come here and get too afraid to stay, even with links and knowing they can be rescued. I don't need the burden of a cowardly companion—I had to see if you could get here alone."

"Well, I have."

"Probably had to dull most of your thoughts to do it."

His face, she thought, might have been handsome if his bones were more delicate; a scowl deformed his features. His eyes were nearly as green as the leaves on the tree limbs that drooped over the grassy roof of his hut. His tanned face was smooth, but his arms and legs were covered with fine brown hairs; coarser curls grew on his chest. She repressed a shudder.

"You're surprised at how ugly I am," he said. "Now you know why I didn't show you an image."

"I wasn't thinking of that."

"Of course you were. People get used to my appearance after a while—it doesn't seem so strange in this context. But it does surprise some when they first see me."

She wondered why he didn't have his body sculpted. Few changes would have been required—a little thinning of the bones and muscles, the removal of some of his body hair, refinement of the strong-featured face. But the man was solitary and might not care how he looked much of the time. Perhaps he even took a little pleasure in startling those who sought him out.

She walked toward him slowly; her nose wrinkled as she smelled his sweat. "Stop right there." He raised his wand. "I'm willing to guide you, but don't get too close to me. You're not used to other people anyway, so it'll be easier if you keep your distance."

Orielna stepped back. "Perhaps you're right," she said haltingly. "My sharer has led a very quiet and removed life."

"You're also like the one you seek, so we'll both be better off if you don't come too close to me."

She winced. "I'm in balance, and if Josef had been, he wouldn't have—" She looked away. "You might have let Aniya and me know more about you, so I'd know how to behave. I'm not sure of how to act with other people. If you'd allow the Net to tell me a little more about you—"

"I'm a hunter and I'll help you. That's all you need to know. Maybe you won't be here that long. Your sharer may get lonely and summon you."

"Aniya's used to being alone, and she had a new eidolon brought to her before I left, a man named Karel." Orielna felt a pang as she thought of her sharer and the eidolon with her now. "He looks a lot like me," she added proudly, "slender and blond, with her black eyes and—"

"The perfect companion, no doubt."

She drew herself up, annoyed at his tone. "I hope your helpmind won't be too disturbed by my presence to tend to me. If you'd rather not have me issue commands to it myself, I'm willing to let you—"

"I have no helpmind here."

She gritted her teeth. He might have warned her of that earlier. How could he bear to live this way? Except for his link, he might almost have been an unchanged man.

Daro gestured at a bundle near his feet. "I'll pitch this tent tonight for myself. You may use the hut—the ditch behind it is the latrine. You should rest for most of the day—we'll have to start early tomorrow."

He stepped aside as she entered the hut. A globe glowed on a wooden platform; shelves of supplies lined the walls and a small hide-covered bed occupied one corner. Orielna slipped off her pack and sat on the bed, glaring at the dirt floor. Maybe she should be grateful he didn't have a helpmind; a nexus with his sullen, unpleasant manner might have been unbearable.

She calmed herself at last and went outside. Daro had already pitched his tent. "You'll find water in the jugs on the shelves," he said. "I fetched it from the stream below—it's safe to drink."

She sat down in front of the hut. His comment was odd; even tainted water would produce only a mild discomfort before her body recovered. Daro swatted at a fly, then seated himself. "Excuse me for mentioning this," she said, "but I thought you hunters only stunned your game, and there's a hide on your bed." Her voice caught. "I can't sleep on a dead animal's skin."

Daro leaned forward. "It was a gift. If you don't want it there, fold it up and put it on a shelf."

Unchanged people must have given it to him; only they would kill an animal. "I see," she said. "I'm a little surprised that you'd want to use it."

"I use what I can."

Orielna shuddered, wondering how she would endure his company. "Have you seen Josef?" she asked. Daro shook his head. "Then where are we to look?"

"I didn't *see* him. I didn't say he hadn't passed this way." His lip curled; his green eyes seemed to be mocking her. He reached into a pocket and held up a slender gold wristband. "Have you seen this before?"

"Josef wore that kind of bracelet," she replied. "But others must have bracelets like it."

"Those who come here usually don't wear such ornaments." He pointed to his right. "Whoever wore it was traveling east—I saw the trail. It's a cold trail now, but we can still search to the east. If he kept moving in that direction, he might have come to a village I know."

"A village?" she asked, staring at his muscular arm.

"Of the unchanged." He was silent for a moment. "Don't look so surprised. You knew we weren't alone in here."

Orielna steadied herself. "How would they have treated him?"

He folded his arms. "They might have welcomed him, or they might have run away from him. It depends on how they felt at the time." He chuckled ominously. "If he didn't conduct himself properly and offended them, or they saw he couldn't protect himself, they might even have killed him, in which case your sharer's problem is solved."

"No," she whispered.

"Who can tell? I speak the villagers' language, and they've never harmed anyone I led there, but it is a possibility. Still, it seems unlikely." His voice was a bit gentler; his face softened a little. "My guess is that he's still alive and that his link would have alerted the Net if he weren't, but I can't be certain. He's apparently roaming around with a completely closed link and might not have had a chance to open it before dying, in which case his body couldn't possibly be revived now."

"I'm aware of that."

"I want to be sure that you know what you're facing. He was a fool to come in here with a closed link. Only someone who knows this Garden well should risk it."

"He wanted to escape completely," she said. "I doubt he was thinking of the danger, and he knows what he'll face if he's found." She tried to compose herself, knowing that she would have to put herself into a deep trance that night in order to sleep. "Daro, I'm afraid. Couldn't you look for him without me? You know the Garden, and I'd only be an impediment. I could wait here for you."

He shook his curly head. "He's your responsibility, not mine. Your sharer sent you here. If you don't stay with me until he's found, Aniya will forfeit any claims she has to decide his fate." He frowned. "She should have come herself instead of sending you." He stood up and lifted the tent flap. "Get some rest. We'll go to that village tomorrow."

Daro was up when she left the hut. He sat by his tent, eyes closed, arms resting on his folded legs, apparently listening to someone through his link. Orielna fidgeted; he opened his eyes.

"Don't let me interrupt you," she said stiffly.

"You didn't interrupt anything."

"I suppose you must have been communicating with your linkmate."

He said, "I have no linkmate."

"How unusual."

"I never had the desire for one," he said. "I don't care to

reveal so much of myself to a person I'm not likely to meet."

"But that's the point," she said. No helpmind, no linkmate—she had never heard of anyone quite like this man. A person as solitary as Daro would need a linkmate even more than others in order to share the thoughts, feelings, and fantasies he could not reveal to most people. Knowing that one would never meet one's linkmate in the flesh made such revelations possible; anything could be confessed to a linkmate. Such a bond was a special one and kept a person's more troubling thoughts apart from the rest of his life.

Aniya's linkmate was a man named Hassan. He had courted her through his link when Aniya had no eidolons, presenting the image of a dark-haired man with warm brown eyes to her. His actual appearance did not matter; the image pleased Aniya, and she had found it easy to share her hidden desires with him. The simulated experiences they summoned through their links were often violent ones, and Hassan was content to be dominated and subdued. It was a perfect bond, and Orielna loved Hassan as much as her sharer did; her memories of Hassan's courtship were as vivid as Aniya's. Orielna suddenly wanted to reach out to Hassan, which surprised her; Aniya did not wish to commune with her linkmate until Josef was found.

I'm beginning to diverge, she thought. She had known that was a possibility when she left Aniya's side. No, she told herself firmly. She only wanted to touch something familiar; if Aniya were here in her place, she would feel the same way.

"Actually," Daro said, "I was listening to some of the minds." She forced her attention back to him. "So few people really communicate with them."

"Why do you say that?" she asked. "People couldn't get through a day without addressing the Net at some point."

"They ask for amusements, or new games, or for little tidbits of information that might enliven a gathering, or for synthetic experiences they wouldn't care to have in real life." His scowl had returned. "The Net could open a world of ideas to us—they've probably even gone beyond what people themselves once knew, but I don't suppose you have the slightest curiosity about that."

"If they can do the thinking better than we can, there's little reason for me to be curious. It's enough to know that they'll care for us." She opened her link a little more, sensing the invisible tendrils that bound her to the Net. The minds were a web of unseen strands, linking the tiny nodes of the mentalities that resided in scanners, dwellings, machines, and people. The link inside her was the center of its own network, one that repaired her damaged cells, attacked viral invaders, healed genetic breaks, strengthened failing arteries and nerves, and drew on endorphins to keep her in balance. The Net of minds maintained her world and the Hoop of Habitats.

Thinking of the Net always comforted Orielna; the minds were her protectors. Yet Josef had closed his link, severing the strand that bound him to the Net. He could not survive that way for long. She had rarely closed her channels completely, and then only when she was near a scanner or a nexus that could watch her and keep her safe. Josef would have to open his link soon, and then she would find him.

"Why did Josef kill that woman?" Daro asked.

The question startled her. "But you know why. Aniya allowed you to experience the entire incident."

"I saw it only from Kitte's perspective. I want to know what you think."

"Kitte was trying to keep him. She'd ordered her helpmind to lock him inside her dwelling with her, and she'd closed her link. He had no way to override her command, so he attacked her out of desperation. In a way, he had no choice."

Daro arched his brows. "No choice? He might have waited. I doubt she would have kept him locked inside forever. He could have soothed her and gone along with her, then made his escape later. It's interesting that you say he had no choice."

"He was frightened. Kitte was babbling about making him her eidolon—she must have seemed overwhelming. He was trapped, with no way out. He wouldn't have attacked her if she'd just left him an escape."

"Interesting response," Daro said. "You're telling me that the only ways he could react were either to run and hide or to attack anything he saw as a threat. He couldn't find another way to handle it."

"He's not used to other people."

"You mean he's terrified of anything he can't control, anything that isn't subject to his will."

"Yes." She thought of Aniya, surrounded by the house that enclosed her courtyard, safe from anything that might disturb her life. "I can't see what good talking about this will do."

"I've learned something about both him and you." Daro rose and slipped his powerful arms through the straps of his pack. "We'll reach the village by this afternoon, provided you can keep up with me. If they've seen Josef, they may be able to tell us where he's headed. He might even be in that village now."

"I hope so," she said.

Daro's mouth twisted. "I hope not. If he is, we may have trouble extricating him."

He led her away from the clearing. She kept a few paces behind him, mindful of his warning not to get too close. The morning air was cool; they had soon left the creek behind, but thick bushes and tangled roots slowed their pace. The hunter studied the ground and scanned the forest as he walked; she realized that he was not relying on his link to guide him.

Gradually, she grew aware of how isolated they were, even with their links. In the world outside the wall, the minds had sensors in every city, dwelling, and vehicle. Every step that took her farther from the wall increased her vulnerability; if she was injured, some time might pass before help could reach her. The minds would be perceiving only what she and Daro saw; there were no sensors among the trees to warn them of danger.

She was now sure that Aniya would not have Josef wiped when he was found; she would keep him with her, however unhappy he became. Orielna pitied Josef for a moment and could almost imagine herself in his place—alone, frightened of what lay around him, desperate to escape the sharer who would imprison him.

She had fallen behind; Daro gestured at her impatiently. She adjusted her pack and pressed on. They might not find Josef at all. If he kept his link closed, they would have to search the Garden for some time. I'd have to stay here, she thought; the possibility made her catch her breath.

She gazed at Daro's brown arms; his muscles tightened as he pushed a tree limb aside. She wondered what it would be like to link with him, what kinds of feelings and memories he might share with her.

She should not be thinking of that, having nothing to offer him except a mind that was a hollow shell made up of Aniya's thoughts. The separation from her sharer was unbalancing her; she had never seen herself that way before. How could she think of growing closer to Daro? Aniya would have been repelled by his strangeness, his difference from herself.

No, she thought; if I'm feeling this, then Aniya would have felt the same thing. I can't be diverging, not yet.

Daro halted and looked back. The hunter would see only Aniya in her, and he already despised her sharer. He would recall what Josef had done and think she was capable of similar deeds. Kitte had called her a shadow. She dulled her thoughts and followed the man.

They reached a river by noon. Orielna kept behind Daro along the bank, then noticed that a few plants had been cut at or trampled. A twig cracked; she started.

Daro stopped and turned toward her. "Someone was watching us," he said. "The villagers will know we're coming now—they're just beyond that bend ahead. Don't speak unless I address you, and do exactly as I do." He paused. "They'll be getting ready to greet two more ghosts."

"Ghosts?"

"Ghosts who come here in human bodies—that's how they see us."

Orielna shook her head. "What a strange idea."

"I don't find it so."

"If they see us that way, then surely they couldn't have harmed Josef." She smiled a little. "After all, if he's seen as a ghost, then they—"

"They think our bodies house spirits. If the spirit offends them, they're capable of striking at it, since killing the body would only send the spirit back to the realm of the dead. Keep that in mind when we meet them."

As they rounded the bend, she heard voices. Five huts stood in a clearing a few paces from the river; three lean-tos made of hides and wood sat near the huts. Six children were playing on the bank; they looked up as she and Daro approached. She thought of the way those children must have entered life—the chance combinations of genes, the gestation inside the bodies of women, the bloody and hazardous process of birth beyond the safety of an ectogenetic chamber and the guidance of the Net.

"Smile," Daro said, "and keep your hands at your sides."

The children ran toward the huts as Orielna and Daro entered the clearing. Five women were seated around a fire; they rose and quickly followed the children into the huts. Eight men lingered near the flames; their hands clutched spears.

"Something's wrong," Daro said softly. "Usually they all run out to greet me."

"Maybe we should leave."

"Do you want to risk a spear in your ribs? Smile. They're more likely to strike out if they see fear."

Two men stepped forward, still holding their spears. They wore loincloths; one had a body as stocky and hard as Daro's, the other a tangled beard heavily streaked with gray. Daro bowed toward the gray-bearded man, and Orielna did the same, averting her eyes from his slightly withered arms and flabby belly. A woman peered out from a hut, her mouth in a grimace, and Orielna saw that she had no front teeth. The village stank with the odors of roasted meat, sweat, and a sickly-sweet smell she did not recognize. Her gorge rose; her jaw tightened, locking her smile into place.

The gray-bearded man uttered a stream of words, then

sat down; his companions quickly took up positions around him. "He'll speak to me now," Daro said as he seated himself; Orielna settled next to him.

The men reeked of fish. Something tugged at Orielna's hair; she tensed. A child had crept up to her and was pulling at her blond locks with one filthy hand. The boy grinned at her, then disappeared into a hut. These people had no links, no way to bring themselves into balance; they were capable of anything.

Daro spoke to the men in what sounded like a series of grunts and cries. The gray-bearded man responded, punctuating his words with wails as he shook his fist at the sky. Daro stopped smiling; the unchanged man fell silent at last.

Daro glanced at Orielna; his pupils were pinpoints in his green eyes. "It seems the eidolon was here," he murmured. "He says the body had black hair and your dark eyes. He says Josef—the cursed specter is what he calls him—is a thief."

Daro said more words in the villagers' tongue, then turned toward her again. "I've told him that the spirit will suffer punishment, but I don't know if he believes me. He says he doesn't want our kind haunting his people. If he hadn't recognized me, we would probably have been driven away. I'll have to warn other hunters, tell them to avoid this village for a while."

Daro reached into his pocket and took out a few jeweled trinkets; the men clawed at them greedily. The graybeard let them gather up the jewels, growled out more words, then spat.

"He's saying," Daro whispered, "that I can't pay him for what he's lost." He stood up, helped Orielna to her feet, and led her away by the arm; her knees shook. "Don't look back."

She expected to feel a spear embed itself in her, and nearly cried out for help through her link. They kept walking until they were past the bend and the village was hidden by the trees. Daro's fingers dug into her; she shook off his grip.

"What did he tell you?" she asked.

"The man who spoke to me is their leader. His daughter found Josef and led him there. He was weak from wandering by then, lost, with no food. The villagers fed him what foods he would accept and gave him shelter. They considered freeing the ghost from a body that seemed such a burden, but the leader's daughter wouldn't allow it—it seems she was quite taken with Josef." Daro was silent for a moment. "Josef crept away one night and took the girl with him."

"But he couldn't have," Orielna objected. "He wouldn't have risked—"

"He took the girl, or else she followed him. The old man went after them alone, finally caught up with them, and pleaded with his daughter to come home. She cursed him and said that she belonged to the ghost, and then Josef fired at him with his wand. When the man came to his senses, they were gone, and he couldn't find their trail—the girl must have covered their tracks. She was his only child. She's run off with a ghost, and the leader will have no descendants to keep his name alive in the village. He calls himself a dead man now."

"But Josef—"

"Josef!" Daro showed his teeth. "Careless people don't belong here. He must have thought he could do as he liked among the unchanged. Maybe he's developed a taste for killing after his encounter with that woman Kitte—he could kill the girl and know she could never be revived."

"No," she said. "He didn't know—he couldn't have understood what that man was trying to tell him."

"He doesn't belong here." Daro's face was taut; she was surprised at the depth of his feeling. "Creatures like Josef aren't people—they're bits and pieces, scraps of others, things that have gotten out of hand and think they have a life of their own."

She was stung. "I'm an eidolon, too."

"Yes, you are. Maybe you understand why he'd want to forget his own emptiness by subjugating another."

The hunter strode on; she hurried after him. "Do you care so much about those people? Then why haven't you led them to the wall? They know you—you could have taken them to a better life and supervised their change, but maybe you'd rather watch them bow to you and accept whatever scraps you choose to give them."

He spun around and raised his hand; she stumbled back, afraid he might strike her. "Do you think I haven't tried to lead them out?" He lowered his arm. "If there were ever a chance of that, Josef's destroyed it. They wouldn't follow me now."

He turned and walked on. She ran after him, struggling to keep up with his rapid pace, fearful of him now, but more afraid of being left alone.

Daro retreated to his tent, leaving the hut to Orielna. He spent his days sitting in the clearing, apparently communing with the minds, or wandering by the creek, staying within sight in case she needed him. She did not dare to probe at his thoughts through her link and was afraid even to speak to him. She felt him watching her whenever she went down to the stream to bathe, but he never followed her.

She found herself unable to dampen her thoughts; they

pricked her even during her calmest, most balanced moments. She was an eidolon, no more than the reflection of a woman who hid from the world. Daro had no reason to offer her any companionship; he saw only another fragment of Aniya trying to pretend it was an individual. Sometimes she caught him staring at her as she moved around the clearing, and wondered if he was waiting for her to leave. He was probably regretting that he had ever offered to help her.

After five days, knowing that she would have to confront him, she composed herself before leaving the hut. Daro was climbing toward his tent from the creek; his curly hair glistened with droplets, and a piece of dark cloth was tied around his waist. He had approached her earlier that day, as though about to speak at last, but had said nothing.

"I must speak to you," she said quickly. He halted in front of her and folded his arms. "Isn't it time we resumed our search?"

"I've been waiting for you to ask about that."

"You might have said so."

"I thought you might need time to recover from your encounter with the unchanged—you obviously didn't find it a pleasant experience." He shook some water from his hair. "I've asked the hunters I know to alert me if Josef's sighted, or if they hear anything about where he might have gone. They won't seize him themselves—they'll leave that to us. I didn't want to subject you to the discomfort of a journey of uncertain duration."

"You could have told me."

"The minds would have told you if you'd asked. I assumed you'd understand that I hadn't given up the search. If I had, I would have asked you to find another to help you." He looked down for a moment. "You can leave the

Garden, Orielna." It was the first time she had heard him say her name. "I could look for him by myself, if you prefer that. It might be easier for you."

He wanted to be rid of her, then. "I have to stay," she said. "I can't leave Josef's fate to someone else."

"You could stay until he's sighted, then depart. I'll make every effort to return him to his sharer unharmed."

She said, "I'd rather stay." He raised his head; his green eyes no longer looked so cold. "Aniya would expect it of me. She wouldn't want me to go before he's found."

"And you have to think of her." His face darkened; his eyes were icy again. "I pity Josef a little, and your sharer, too, but I'm sorriest for you."

"There's no need to be," she responded, surprised at how unhappy he sounded. "You puzzle me, Daro. You commune with the minds so much, and yet you often seem just a bit unbalanced. You ought to allow your link to—"

"I don't care to feel like a puppet."

"That's an odd way to look at it," she said.

"I'd rather have my own feelings than ones given to me by something else."

"I don't see the distinction. When they're imparted to you, don't they become your feelings then?"

"How interesting that you, an eidolon with no feelings of your own, would say that."

"Daro—" She paused. The sky was growing dark, and she was suddenly afraid of being alone. "Will you share a meal with me?"

He did not answer. She backed toward the hut. He hesitated, then followed her inside. She seated herself on the dirt floor as he took a package and jug from one shelf.

He sat down and handed her a piece of bread. His face seemed gentler in the soft light of the nearby globe. "You must miss Aniya," he said. "She might have linked with you for the search. It would have been easier for you. You must be anxious to return to her."

She would go back to Aniya because she had nowhere else to go. Aniya's house would close around her; she had never thought of it as a prison before.

"Sometimes," he went on, "I wonder at the cruelty of people who ask for eidolons. They want a world where they're endlessly reflected, where nothing outside them can intrude and remind them of their own limits. They want power over others, but are too cowardly to contend with those unlike themselves. So they ask for eidolons, creatures that can be their children, lovers, friends, servants, and slaves, as well as being mirrors of their minds. And they keep their pets close so that they diverge as little as possible. They'd rather forget that they themselves are no more than the pets of their artificial intelligences."

"The minds can't think of us that way."

"How would you know? We'd rather think of the Net as our servant. I've communed with the minds. I suspect they view us in much the way people see the unchanged—as relics of something they've transcended. Our minds could have grown along with theirs, but they haven't. If they could feel disappointment, they might be disappointed in us."

"There's no reason for them to be," Orielna said. "And you're wrong about Aniya—she isn't cruel."

"You know what Josef's done, yet you say that. The potential for such deeds must lie in her, too."

"He'd diverged after being away from her. He wasn't in balance. He—" Against her will, she found herself recalling the scenarios Aniya experienced with her linkmate Hassan. They were always the same. Aniya would be fleeing from

Hassan, or he would pursue her, but the scene always ended in his submission, his acceptance of any simulated torments or delights she forced upon him. Aniya always shared the experiences with Orielna and Josef afterward. Now, for the first time, Orielna felt that she had always hated those scenarios, that she had experienced them only because Aniya compelled it, and that her pleasure in them was only the shadow cast by her sharer's emotions.

She glanced toward the entrance, noticing that Daro had left her access to it. He was, she supposed, thinking of Josef's panic at being trapped with Kitte, and making sure her own fears weren't roused.

Daro picked up the jug and poured wine into two cups. "What was Aniya's life like before she had you and Josef created?" he asked.

"She lived alone. She had her linkmate—Hassan."

"Is that all? Did she have an earlier life?"

"Yes," Orielna replied. "She loved a man named Piro, and then they separated. I don't know what their life together was like."

"But you have her memories."

"She erased her life with Piro after they parted. He saw her only once after she moved into her present house. She remembered only that she had been with him once—she didn't want to retain anything else. It must have hurt him deeply when he learned she'd wiped all that—she'd escaped him completely, you see."

"How careless of her." Daro lowered his cup. "You're her eidolon, yet she's left you ignorant of part of her life, which means there are things about both her and yourself you can't know. You should have insisted on having those memories." He sipped his wine. "But you couldn't have done that. You're too much like her. I don't suppose you even thought of contacting this Piro and asking him about her. She erased her memories and escaped that man, and now Josef's hiding from her." He shook his head. "Poor Orielna. She's made you her shadow when she may be no more than a shadow herself."

"Don't pity me because of what I am."

"I pity others, not just you. People who wipe their minds, dull any unpleasant feeling, who can't distinguish between their true memories and ones the minds have imparted to them—they all seem like eidolons to me. Maybe that's all your sharer was, and that's why she had her earlier memories wiped. Maybe Josef didn't diverge as much as you think—he may be more like her than she realizes. They may both be fleeing from what they are."

Her heart fluttered. She thought of the image of Piro she had glimpsed when linking with Aniya, with eyes as black as her sharer's and her own. Orielna's sharer had retained only the memory of their last meeting, when Aniya had told Piro she no longer recalled their life together. Piro's unhappy eyes might have been Aniya's when Josef was leaving her.

"Do you want to go back to Aniya?" Daro asked.

"I have to stay until we find Josef."

"I didn't ask that." He leaned toward her. "I asked if you want to go back."

"I don't know." She thought of her sharer. "Daro, I don't know! I'm Aniya's—I can't be feeling this way!"

"Josef was hers as well."

"What's happening to me? When I think of returning to her now—" Her hands shook; she set down her cup.

"You're not Aniya's now, and you won't admit it." He moved closer to her and began to stroke her hair. Someone other than Aniya and her eidolons was touching her; a man was looking at her without seeing her sharer. What did he see? Was there anything inside her that might be her own, that she could share with him?

"Aniya loved Piro," she whispered. "It must have made her suffer, or she wouldn't have erased it."

"I'm not Piro, and you're not Aniya, not now. You might have been diverging even before you left her, and afraid to admit it to yourself then. She knew what she was risking when she sent you here." He cupped her face in his hands. "Orielna, we may be here for a long time. We may never find Josef. He might already be dead—he has only that girl to help him. Couldn't we find some joy together while we wait?"

She curled her fingers around a bit of his hair. "I don't know."

"What you have with me can be yours—yours, not anyone else's. I've wanted to find someone, but when others find out what I am, they retreat. I told myself I was content with solitude and my link, but it isn't so."

"How can I ever know you?" she said quietly.

He held her hands for a moment, then released her. "You have to see what I am. If you want to leave afterward, I won't stop you." He took a breath. "I came out of this Garden—I was once an unchanged man. I followed a visitor to the wall, and he guided me to the life outside it. He was kind, almost like a father, but he soon tired of me and his friends kept watching me for signs of wildness. They saw me as a freak, or an amusement—not as a man. I knew I'd have to return here then."

"You might have erased your memories," she said. "You could have started over and become like everyone else. It wouldn't have mattered what you once were after that—you wouldn't remember it."

"I couldn't do it—that seemed too much like dying. I'm

still primitive enough to fear what might have happened to my soul."

His confession, to her surprise, did not frighten or repel her. Whatever he had been, he was whole; he had retained painful memories to keep himself whole.

"I thought I might have a purpose here," Daro continued. "After my change, I wondered why the minds allowed the unchanged to suffer and die here. It came to me then that, however cruel it seemed, there was wisdom in maintaining a strain of humanity untouched by the Net. They're what we once were, and perhaps only they can one day develop along another way. Anyone who's brave enough to abandon the Garden and all that he knows might someday be brave enough to look beyond Earth and the Habitats—to join the minds as a partner in discovering what can be known."

He gazed past her. "I hoped to lead others outside," he went on. "I knew the problems they'd face in adapting to a world where they'd see the minds as gods and themselves as blessed. It can be a shock to realize that even a paradise can pall. But the unchanged fear the world outside too much. They see the world beyond the wall as death's realm, and its people as ghosts. Perhaps they're not far wrong." Daro sighed. "I came from that village you saw, although everyone I knew in my former life is long dead. I can't truly be part of the Garden, and yet I can't live in your world, either."

"Maybe you can," she heard herself say, "with me."

"You know what it'll mean for you. Don't reach out to me and then retreat."

"I won't retreat."

His eyes widened with hope. She began to explore him with her hands, thinking of the strangeness that might open itself to her. In the dim light of the hut, Daro's eyes, with their enlarged pupils, seemed almost as black as her own. He helped her out of her shirt and pants, then stretched out on the dirt floor, drawing her to him.

This act could only take her farther away from her sharer. She opened another channel and called out to him through her link. "No," he whispered, gripping her tightly around her waist. "No linking, no images to help you along. Close it, Orielna—be alone with me."

His hands kept surprising her. There had been no surprises with Aniya or Josef, who had always known what she wanted, but she welcomed his unfamiliarity. His body had the fresh scent of the stream. She closed her link and pressed her lips to his.

Daro knelt by the creek, a few paces upstream from where they had washed, and filled a jug with water. He glanced toward Orielna and smiled, and she wondered how she had ever thought of him as ugly.

They had already explored much of the land around the clearing; Daro had pointed out an animal trail and shown her a few of the plants the unchanged gathered for food. Perhaps they would follow the deer today; Daro knew of a place by the stream where the animals often came to drink. Their hikes seemed to make it easier for him to speak of his former life. While showing her various herbs and telling her of their uses, he had talked of the mother who had brewed herbal tea for him. The song of a bird had evoked a story about the first time he had hunted with his father.

Sometimes he began to speak, then fell silent, and she sensed that he was recalling unhappier times. "I have to remember," he had told her one evening. "I can't rid myself of the feeling that if I forget, the spirits of my parents and all the souls of the people I knew will vanish."

They had not linked, and she knew she was not ready to let the Net impart his past to her directly, or to view herself through his eyes. That would have to come when her sense of herself was stronger. Only last night, she had felt a sudden panic that she might lose herself, after all, that Daro might swallow her until she was no more than his reflection. He had held her, soothing her as she talked until her fear passed.

Daro pushed a stopper into his jug, stood up, and walked toward her. He always lay on his side, or under her, whenever they made love, as if he feared that she might feel threatened otherwise. The air was still; Daro had mentioned that a storm was on the way. They would retreat to the hut then and wait for it to pass.

Daro reached for her hand as she got to her feet. "Do you have any regrets?" he asked.

"No."

He kissed her; she looped her arms around his waist. He always let her explore him, guiding her hands and lips as she rediscovered every part of him before opening herself to his touch. Everything she felt with him was hers now; she no longer felt troubled by thoughts of Josef and Aniya. If she never found Josef, they would each have what they sought; he would stay hidden, and she would remain with Daro. Aniya would have her eidolon Karel to console her for her loss.

Daro tensed; she let go of him. "Someone wants to speak to us," he said; she had already sensed the call through her own link. He set down his jug as Orielna opened another channel.

The image of a dark-skinned man with golden eyes appeared in front of them. He wore a brown shirt and pants, with a wand at his waist, and carried a pack. "Greetings, Nedeeb," Daro said.

"Greetings. I have a message for you and this woman. I've seen the one you seek." Orielna drew in her breath. "I would have stunned him myself," the dark-skinned hunter continued, "and had him brought to you. Frankly, I dislike leaving him to roam with a closed link, but the Net informed me that you still wished to take him yourself. I don't much care what happens to him, but that's his sharer's responsibility, not mine. I'm only concerned with the danger he may pose to others as he is."

"Where is he?" Daro asked.

"From where you stand, a few days' travel directly east. I saw him on the shore of the lake there. I didn't recognize him at first—he seemed like an unchanged man—but he was carrying a wand and resembled the image I'd been shown. A young woman was with him. He didn't see me."

"Are you certain it's Josef?" Orielna asked.

The image turned its head toward her. "Ask the minds to show you what I saw."

She opened another channel. A dark-haired man was gazing at an expanse of white-capped water. The wind whipped his hair; he turned slightly and she saw Josef's black, tormented eyes, then closed the channel abruptly. "I've seen enough."

"He struck the woman," Nedeeb said. "I nearly aimed at him then, but she seemed able to defend herself, and I wasn't about to go to the trouble of a capture for the sake of an unchanged woman." His eyes narrowed. "Will you pursue him?"

Daro's face was grim. "I don't know yet."

"If you decide not to go, I'll go back and take him myself. The hunt might prove interesting, and I'll see that he's under restraint before he's returned to his sharer, but if he causes me too much trouble—" The hunter shrugged.

Orielna said, "We'll go after him, of course."

Daro glanced at her. She was suddenly conscious of how her image must look to Nedeeb, and sorry she had unthinkingly allowed the Net to show her as she was. Her long blond hair was tangled and ungroomed, her shirt and pants stained and wrinkled; she looked as wild as Josef, and felt shame.

"Safe hunting," Nedeeb said. The image faded and then vanished.

Daro sat down and stared at the creek. She should have known their time together could not last, that the bonds tying her to Josef and Aniya would tug at her again. She had been wallowing in her dream, forgetting her purpose.

"We don't have to go to him," Daro said. "I can tell Aniya where he is. You could try to persuade her to let Nedeeb take him—it sounds as if he'd enjoy the opportunity. She could ask other hunters to bring him to her."

"She wouldn't want that—it's pointless to consider it. I have to speak to him myself. We'll leave right away."

He looked up at the darkening sky. "It's going to rain. You wouldn't like hiking through a storm."

"Tomorrow, then. We can't wait—someone else might see him and decide to act, or he might flee the area."

"And what will you do if we find him?" he asked.

"I'll try to convince him to return willingly. If he won't, I suppose we'll have to summon help and force him to come with us."

"And after that?"

Her hands fluttered. "I'll have to go back to Aniya with him. They'll both need me."

He said, "You'd rather be a fragment, after all, her reflection again—that way, you needn't risk anything or make your own decisions. I was a fool to think you could be anything else."

"Don't let it trouble you. Wipe your memories if the thought of me disturbs you so much."

"You still don't understand, do you? I was willing to wait until you truly became yourself. I didn't want you running away from me the way Josef's running from everything, the way your sharer hides from the world. It's something the unchanged learn early, how to wait—it's something all hunters have to learn, but we're always aware that waiting might not gain us anything in the end. Few people beyond the wall ever learn that, but then they don't really have to, do they?"

She sank to the ground and reached for him; he pushed her away violently. "Don't, Orielna. I'll be relieved to see you go." His green eyes were again those of a stranger.

The wind wailed as rain pelted the ground. Orielna lay on Daro's bed, listening to the storm; the hunter was stretched out on the floor with his back to her.

Aniya would link with her when she returned, and her memories of Daro would become her sharer's as well. Aniya would see that Orielna had diverged, and that would cause her some pain. But perhaps she had not deviated very much; when Aniya saw Daro through Orielna's eyes, she might come to love him, too. She might content herself with simulated sessions featuring the man, but perhaps she would also risk coming to the Garden to see him. Orielna would become no more than another part of Aniya to him. Why shouldn't he love Aniya? Orielna was only a mind made in her sharer's image.

No, she told herself fiercely; I'm not that anymore.

"Daro," she murmured. He did not reply. "Daro." Her link told her that he was awake, but she would have known that anyway; his breathing was uneven, his muscles tensed. "I'll take Josef back, and then I'll tell Aniya I'm leaving her. She has the right to decide what happens to Josef after what he's done, but she can't hold me."

"You say that now." She had to strain to hear him above the steady pattering of the rain. "It'll be harder to say it to her. She'll find ways to keep you from leaving, and after you've linked with her again, you may not want to go."

"I won't link with her. She can find out what she needs to know from the Net, but my thoughts of you will be mine. I will leave her, Daro."

He did not speak. He had said that he was used to waiting. He would wait to see her demonstrate that she meant what she said. She would have to become herself without knowing if she could return to him, if he would welcome her once more. She had entered the realm of uncertainty that her sharer feared so much.

Orielna kept up with Daro, but he stayed a few paces in front of her, as he had when they had first met. He retreated into silence and did not speak even when they stopped to rest. At night, she slept inside his small tent while he lay by a fire outside.

She kept her thoughts dulled, heedless of the landscape around her. In balance, her feelings for Daro were muted, bringing only a faint twinge of regret. She would not give him the chance to strike back at her by pleading with him before he rejected her utterly. His memory would fade inside her, and she could always have it erased. They would find Josef; she refused to think of what might happen after that.

Her nights were dreamless periods of oblivion. During the days, the forest seemed misty; she trudged through the fog in a trance, her eyes focused on Daro's back. He was only another shadow in the mist, almost as insubstantial as the woods. When he stopped, she halted; when he changed course, she followed him.

Daro stopped suddenly and held up his hand. Through the mist, she dimly noticed that they were now among hills where the trees were not as thick. She came to herself, her mind suddenly alert; the mist cleared.

Two unchanged people stood at the top of a hill. The man and the woman each carried a spear; Orielna's hand moved toward her wand as Daro called out to them.

The man shouted a few words, set down his spear, and stretched out his empty hands. Daro nodded; the stranger stooped to pick up his weapon, then disappeared over the hill with the woman.

"What did you say?" Orielna asked. "What do they want?"

"They've invited us to join them. I trust you can conduct yourself properly."

"Do you think we should?"

"They might have seen Josef. We're not that far from the lake now."

"Then I'll try not to offend them," she said.

They climbed the hill, descended the other side, and came to a hollow. The unchanged couple sat near a fire. The man was broad-shouldered and blond, the woman smaller and darker. Daro led Orielna toward them, sat down and took off his pack, then offered them some of his food. The woman giggled as she pulled at the wrappings, holding them to one small bare breast as if they were an ornament. Small bones were scattered by the fire; Orielna felt sick. The man was holding out what looked like the burned limb of an animal.

Daro took the food and nibbled at it as she tried to steady herself. The couple smiled as they ate, leaning toward each other to exchange pieces of food. Age had not marred their handsomeness yet; the minds might have shaped their bodies. They would not have their youthfulness for long; she wondered how aware they were of that. Orielna thought of the days she had spent with Daro, believing they would not end.

The two spoke with Daro for a little while, then stood up and bowed. The hunter's face was solemn as he watched them walk away. "They're returning to their people," he said. "We can sleep here tonight—it'll be dark soon."

"Did they see Josef?"

He shook his head. "He may still be near the lake, though. Those two haven't been there, and they don't seem too concerned with anything around them anyway. They're in love, you see—they recently built their dwelling together. They asked me if we were the ghosts of anyone they had known."

"Do you ever wish—" She paused. "Do you ever regret your change?"

Daro smiled a little. "Of course not. How can I regret that I didn't age and die? What I miss is quite simple, really—the feeling that my life has some meaning to others besides myself. That couple has that—they know how short-lived their joy will be and how precarious their life is. Every moment of joy they can give to each other or to those they love is a victory."

"Did you love someone before you went to the wall?"

A rasping sound came from his throat; he covered his face. She should not have asked that; it would only push him into silence again.

He lowered his arm, picked up a stick, and poked at the dying flames. "There was a girl," he said softly. "We used to talk of going to the wall together, but I knew she'd never follow me. I questioned everything, and she used to chide me for it. We were to build a hut together, but I left my village to follow a visitor to the wall. I thought I'd be proving that what my people believed was wrong, that I'd win some sort of glory for myself by entering death's realm and returning from it. I saw myself going back to the village in triumph, with a tale that would make my name live forever and a few baubles to demonstrate its truth."

He took a breath. "The man guided me through the gate. Before I knew it, I was with him inside a flyer, soaring over the earth. My terror was so great I believed my soul had already left my body. I fainted and came to in a room of lights."

"A biogenesis chamber," she said, thinking of the one where she had been formed.

"I thought I was dead and that this place would be either my reward or my punishment. I slept while the minds and their machines labored over my body and implanted my link. The man who brought me out took me to his house. At first, I saw it as a paradise, where my every wish was granted and the gods who loved me spoke inside my head. It took me many years to understand what this new world actually was. By the time I was able to comprehend that I was still alive, I also knew that everyone I had ever loved in the Garden was dead. I'd been outside the wall too long and had become a kind of ghost, after all."

She touched his arm; he did not pull away. "I went back to my village eventually," he continued. "People who hadn't been born when I left were already old. They told me a story about a young man who had dared to follow a ghost to the wall only to be captured by the specter. They also spoke of a young woman who mourned for him, prayed for his soul, then tried to follow him in the only way she could. Her people found her body by the river, where she had taken her own life."

Orielna let out a small cry, horrified by the tale. Could someone love so much?

"Now you know why I belong here. I have this foolish dream, you see, of somehow atoning for what happened by persuading others to leave the Garden with me—not just one or two, but a group, a village, a community of people, brave ones who could accept the Net's gifts and maybe seek to make something more of their lives. They'd have their loved ones with them always, and never see them die. They wouldn't have to be as solitary as I am."

"But you don't have to be—"

"We've spoken enough." The distant look returned to his eyes. "I'll set up the tent and look for more wood." He turned away as he opened his pack.

A shaft of light pierced the darkness. "Wake up," a voice said inside her. Orielna was immediately alert; she clutched at her blanket, then sat up. Daro had called out to her through a channel, she realized, but the gray light outside the open tent flap seemed more like twilight than dawn.

Before she could reply, a dark shape hid the light; a hand reached in and seized her by the wrist. "Close your link," Daro muttered. "Now!"

She closed all the channels, shrinking into herself. "What is it?"

"Josef may be near. I think he might have been following us. I saw the footprints in a patch of muddy ground when I went for wood."

"How do you know they're his?" she asked.

"They were made by boots. They aren't yours, and I'm wearing moccasins, and the unchanged don't have boots. There aren't any hunters or visitors near us, either—the Net verified that." He pulled her outside; she scrambled to her feet. "Until we know what he's after, we can't let him track us through his link."

"But it's closed," she said. "He wouldn't chance opening it now, and if he did, we'd know where he is."

"He might risk it for an instant." Daro pulled the stakes from the ground, then folded the tent and blanket quickly. "And consider this—there's no one around who could reach us very soon. If we had to be rescued, it would take some time for a flyer to reach us from the wall. We have to make ourselves as invisible to him as possible."

"But if you think we're in danger, that's more reason to stay linked to the Net. The minds can't help us if we drop out now."

"Listen to me!" He stood up, lifted the pack to his back, and attached the straps across his bare chest. "A lot could happen to us before help gets to us. We have to rely on ourselves now." He took her by the arm. "Come."

He had already thrown dirt on the fire. They hastened away from the clearing toward a wooded hill. Daro let go of her and took out his wand as they began to climb. When they were halfway up the hill, he halted and dropped the pack next to her.

"Stay here," he whispered. "Keep your wand ready. Don't shoot unless you have no choice—the beam will give you away. I'll be back for you when I'm sure it's safe."

She nodded, too frightened to speak. He crept up the hill, keeping low, and was lost among the trees. Orielna crouched behind a shrub; something snarled in the distance. The wand shook in her hand; she swallowed hard. How long had Josef been tracking them? She gripped the wand tightly, ready to shoot.

She was stiff with tension when she saw a dark form descending the hill, and recognized Daro. He hurried toward her and picked up the pack. "Follow me," he said softly, "but stay down."

He climbed in a crouch, his wand out, looking like a large beetle with the hump of the pack on his back. Orielna kept low as she climbed after him. At the top of the hill, there was a gap among the sparse trees marked by a low wall made of tree trunks.

Daro helped her over the wall, then settled her in one corner. The space inside was small, the ground matted with dead leaves and pine needles. Daro moved around the space, staying low as he peered over the wall, then came back to her.

"We're lucky we found this place," he said. "I don't think he's near us now, but I can't be sure—he could be anywhere below us. Still, he can't reach us without being seen."

She knelt and peered over the stacked tree trunks. Anyone approaching them would have to cross the small open space that divided the wall from the trees just below it. "What is this place?" she asked.

"It must have been a fortress of some kind. In a battle, high ground can give you an advantage."

"The unchanged still fight?"

"Sometimes."

"You'd think that, with their lives so short as it is, they wouldn't rush to end them that way." She rested a hand on the wall. Now that she was safe, at least temporarily, her earlier fears seemed groundless. "He may simply want to talk to us. He couldn't mean to harm me."

"Are you so certain? You know what he did to Kitte, and he'll know you're here to see that he atones for that." He paused. "I should have known he was following us, I should have sensed it. You have to know when something might be tracking you here. I would have felt him watching us if I hadn't been so distracted thinking about you."

"I wasn't aware that you were."

"You should have left the Garden when you had the chance. I could have hunted him alone and been free of you."

"Daro, we could ask for help now. It doesn't matter if Josef learns where we are—we could hold out long enough for other hunters to reach us, and then—"

"No."

"They could help us find him."

"No!" He moved away from her. "I mean to find him myself now, and you're so sure he'll listen to you. He might not if you ask others to join the hunt." He sighed. "You can still leave if you're afraid. Touch the Net and summon a flyer—I'll wait with you until it arrives. Go back to Aniya and leave Josef to me."

"I can't," she whispered. She couldn't tell what she feared more—returning to her sharer and admitting that she had given up the search, or leaving Daro alone to hunt the eidolon. Josef might not harm him as long as Daro was with her, but alone, Daro might not be safe. She wanted to say so, but would only anger him by implying that he could not look out for himself. "Aniya's hoping I can reach him somehow, that he'll return to her peaceably. I can't let her down."

"Of course not," he said mockingly. "It might make it harder for you to return to being her reflection."

"I know why you're so anxious to find him. It's a challenge to you now—you can't bear the thought that your prey might escape. You're embarrassed that he was able to trail you and that you didn't—"

"Be silent." His fingers dug into her shoulder painfully. "You and your sharer brought me into this, and I'll see it settled. You'll watch from this side—I'll guard the other. I doubt he'll come up here, if he's still anywhere nearby, but we might as well be prepared." He released her.

The Moon had risen; its green orb shimmered in the east. The tiny lights of the Hoop that ringed the Earth shone steadily. She thought of all the times she had gazed at the heavens with Aniya; how strange that the sky still looked much the same when so much inside her had changed. She gripped her wand and turned her attention to the hillside below.

Daro left the enclosure at dawn to scout the land below, then climbed back to her. "I saw his tracks," he said. "He went south—I followed them for a bit. It's odd—he didn't conceal them and kept to softer ground where he was sure to leave a trail. I can't believe he wouldn't have learned something about covering his tracks from that unchanged girl, so he must expect us to follow them."

Orielna frowned. "Maybe he was just trying to get away from us. He wouldn't have been thinking of what tracks he was leaving if he was in a hurry."

"The prints showed he was moving slowly. The girl might have shown him how to set a trap. I think he may want to lead us away from the lake, which is exactly why we should head there now." A note of contempt had crept into his voice. "When he goes back, we could be waiting for him."

"He might have moved from that region by now," she said.

"But he has no reason to do so. He didn't see Nedeeb and probably hasn't guessed that we know he was sighted there. All he knows is that we're out here searching for him. He'd expect us to follow the trail if we hadn't known he was seen at the lake."

She tried to imagine herself inside Josef's mind; that had been so simple for her once. Maybe it had all become a game to him by now, with his mind as unbalanced as it was. "Then let's go," she said.

They descended the hill's eastern slope; she kept her wand in her hand as she walked. Lack of sleep would not affect them for a while; even with closed links, the molecular systems implanted in their bodies would clear the physical residues of fatigue. Eventually, however, they would have to sleep; their minds required dreams to keep in balance.

At the bottom of the hill, the trees closed in around them. Birds chirped above them, then abruptly lapsed into silence. The darkness of the woods made her uneasy; her neck prickled.

Daro halted and said, "Don't move." She wondered why she could no longer hear the birds overhead. Daro suddenly pushed her to one side and aimed his wand toward the sky. A beam shot out from a bough, catching the hunter in the chest; he toppled forward slowly. Orielna raised her wand. A flash of light blinded her—

She was lying on her back, with something cold and sharp pressed against her throat. "Don't open your link," a familiar voice said. "I know it's closed—I checked before. Told the Net I was going to meet you and give myself up after I had a chance to talk to you. I'm closed now, but don't think you can call out for help. If I even suspect you are, you can suffer quite a lot before help reaches you."

Orielna opened her eyes. Josef was kneeling over her, gripping her by the hair; he held up a knife in his other hand. "But you won't try to touch the Net now, will you?" he said. "You don't want to get hurt. You wouldn't want your friend to suffer."

"Daro," she gasped. Her headache was fading; she sat up. The hunter lay on his stomach, his arms and legs bound with torn pieces of blanket. His face was turned toward her, eyes closed. Blood trickled from a wound in his head. "What have you done to him?"

"I hit him harder than I intended when he came to. He looked quite angry before I struck him. He's still breathing."

She had to open her link. But Josef would know if she did; he would see it in her eyes and expression. She could not risk it, not with Daro lying there helpless. She noticed then that Josef had disarmed them; their wands were under his belt, next to his own.

"What do you want?" she said.

"Why, to talk to you, of course. Isn't that why you came after me, to persuade me to go back to Aniya? If she'd wanted me wiped or destroyed, she could have sent someone else. We'll talk, but not here. We'll leave this man behind."

"You won't leave him there like that."

"He'll come to before long, and if he needs help, he can call for it. He'll want to hold out for a while, though—how humiliating it would be for him, letting his fellow hunters know that I was able to overcome him."

She would summon help. There had to be a way to do it. Whatever Josef did to her, Daro would be safe.

"You seem very concerned for him," Josef said. "It must have been pleasant for you, having that amusement, maybe even hoping that he might become yours. You're probably thinking that you can alert the Net when we're away from here. I wouldn't try that, Orielna. He may have to call for help himself, but he'll never forgive you for it. He'll hate you for shaming him."

She stretched an arm toward Daro, then let it fall.

"I see I guessed correctly," Josef said. "The man must have some pride. He'll sacrifice it to save his life if necessary, but he'll never forgive you if you humiliate him by asking the minds to rescue him. And you couldn't bear that, losing the only one who ever saw you as yourself. Oh, what a novel experience that must have been for you."

"You don't know anything about it."

"But I do," he replied. "You are like me, after all. I'm a little disappointed that you walked into my trap so easily. I thought you'd follow the tracks—not that they would have led you to anything—but I was waiting in case you didn't. I knew you wouldn't come this way unless you knew where I was likely to be. When I saw you, I realized you'd been heading for the lake all along." He chuckled. "I thought you might stay up on that hill. I'm sure you would have if you'd been alone, but your hunter friend wouldn't give up the chase so easily."

He was babbling, sounding completely unbalanced. His black hair hung around his face, his skin was darker, his elbows grimed with dirt; his gray pants and shirt were tattered.

"Why are you doing this?" she asked.

Josef laughed. "Because it amuses me. Because I have nothing to lose doing whatever I want to you." He slipped his knife under his belt, trained his wand on her, then dragged her to her feet. "Come along."

"Don't leave him here without a wand."

"He can always ask for help."

"He's unconscious—at least wait until he comes to."

His wand struck the side of her head. She staggered, waiting for the pain to pass. "I could have killed him," he said. "I will if we don't leave now. You'd wail for help from the minds then, but I'd make sure they wouldn't find much. A brain can be crushed—that's all I'd have to do." His booted foot moved closer to Daro's head. "All he'd ever be afterward is an eidolon with a new body and painful restored memories of shame he'd probably choose to erase. You'd lose him for good."

Orielna struggled for breath.

"Are you coming along quietly," Josef said in a softer voice, "or do I have to take firmer measures? I knew she'd send you, that she'd never come herself, but that's all right. We can talk, you and I."

She had loved him once, had seen herself in him. He couldn't have killed it all. "I'll go with you," she said. "I won't open my link. Just don't hurt Daro anymore."

He pushed her forward, prodding her with his wand. "We don't have far to go. The land slopes just ahead—keep going downhill and we'll reach the lake before dark."

She moved on shaky legs. The dizziness she had felt after he struck her was gone, but her head still ached. Her link would soon remedy that, but she could not dull her mind enough to ignore the pain without opening herself to the Net. She would have to endure the discomfort until the damage was repaired.

Josef might be wrong about Daro. The hunter might open his link fully, if only to dampen his pain. He would summon help for her, whatever shame that might bring to him.

"You'll behave yourself," Josef said behind her, "and you'll do as I say, or you'll learn just how much you can be hurt before you're repaired."

"I thought you wanted to talk."

"Oh, but I do. We'll have a nice talk, but remember that I can find other ways to amuse myself with you—that is, if you don't behave."

She had lived this before, she realized, although not exactly in this way, when trapped inside one of the fantasies Aniya employed with her linkmate Hassan. But now she was cast in Hassan's role, which she had never played before—the victim, the one to be subdued—and could not escape simply by closing a channel.

Perhaps Josef was so unbalanced now that nothing around him had any more substance than a fantasy. He was capable of hurting her and would expect her to fear that more than anything. She would make him believe that she was completely cowed, then find a way to escape and summon help.

The sun was low behind them when they reached the lake. Josef led her over the rocks along the shore until they came to a lean-to of hides and wooden poles in a clearing overlooking the rocky beach.

"This is how you live?" Orielna said.

He jabbed her with the wand, bruising a rib. "Careful, Orielna. I don't like your tone."

"I'm concerned for you, Josef. You can't go on this way."

"But I can. My link will heal me, and the few unchanged people near here avoid this particular spot now. They're afraid of me, you see."

They climbed up to the makeshift shelter. "Sit down,"

he said, then rummaged through a pack under the lean-to. He held up a leather thong and a piece of rope. "Put your hands behind your back."

"Don't bind me."

"I don't want you tempted to run away and go looking for that friend of yours. You *were* thinking of doing that." He bound her arms, then tied her legs at the ankles.

"He'll come after you," she said.

"Perhaps. I'm curious to see what he does. He'll be a little unbalanced when he comes to himself—he may blame you for his predicament. He might think you've gotten just what you deserve or that you want me now. I'm sure you told him how much we once meant to each other. He may come after me, or he may decide to forget this whole unhappy episode."

Her eyes stung; she closed them for a moment. "You must listen to me," she said. "Aniya wants you back. She won't have you wiped—she only wants you to recover."

"You think so?" he responded. "She'd be so repulsed by me now that erasing me would be her only alternative. She'd never be able to endure my presence again, knowing that I preferred even what I have here to her. I know what I am now—I can't be hers again. But maybe you've diverged so much from her yourself that you can't see that."

"Why did you kill Kitte?"

He laughed softly as he sat down next to her. "She tried to keep me, kept babbling about how I might become her eidolon. She found me in the Garden, just inside the gate. She liked to go there—she imagined that some unchanged person might follow her out and become hers completely, but she didn't have the courage to wander far from the wall."

"You didn't have to—"

"What did I kill?" he asked. "I knew what other people were then—I'd encountered enough of them after I left our sharer. They're nothing but the thoughts others give them, or the memories the minds feed them—they're shells of sensations with nothing inside. Kitte was like all the others—that's what I was thinking when my hands were around her throat. There was nothing inside her to kill, nothing that was truly hers, but that wasn't the only reason I wrung the life from her body. I knew I was doing something that was truly mine, that the minds hadn't put inside me."

"You've gone wrong, Josef. You can't—"

"I'm myself for the first time. If you'd been among other people more, you would have seen what we are. We're nothing but puppets of the minds. They probe our thoughts and soothe us so that we never know what we are, and never truly reveal themselves to us. They know we're too limited ever to be more. Humankind built itself a trap when the minds were created—they wanted intelligence that could grasp what few human minds could encompass. Now they give us what we want so that we'll forget we've been surpassed, that nothing will ever be truly ours again."

"The minds give us what we choose to accept." She thought of what Daro had told her their first night together. "There might be more for us if we had the courage to reach for it."

"You mean they might grant us a few more gifts if we begged for them, and then we'd lose even more of ourselves. No, Orielna—I'll stay as I am. I won't be Aniya's puppet, or the Net's. I know what I am now, and I accept it—I won't hide from it the way the rest of you do."

She moved her hands, straining against the thong; her wrists were bound tightly. "Come away with me, Josef. Aniya only wants you safe—she may be content to let you live in her house without communing with her."

"How false! You don't believe that. Anyway, there's someone else here to consider besides me."

"That unchanged girl," she said. "I was wondering about her. I thought she might have left you."

"So you know about her. She can't leave me—she's abandoned her people, and there's nowhere else for her to go. Right now, she's probably fishing at the river near here. She hunts for me, catches fish, and looks for plants. The rest of the time, she jabbers at me in that speech of hers. I've learned just enough of it to tell her what to do, and I won't teach her our language. It's amusing to watch her trying to sort out my words while her eyes plead with me to say just one word she can understand."

"We'll bring her along," Orielna said. "I'll ask Aniya to have you help her through her change."

He glared at her. "Why do you keep talking about impossibilities?" He shook back his hair. "She's mine. She won't know anything of the outside world except what I choose to reveal to her. She wouldn't remain mine for long out there." He grinned, showing his teeth. "You don't want to go back yourself. Aniya will make certain you never leave her again. You fear that—I know. We still share, you and I."

"Less than you think."

He grabbed her hair, forced her head back, and clawed at her shirt. "Behave yourself." He fumbled between her legs. "I've always known how to please you before, haven't I?"

She heard a cry. Josef let go; she looked up. A young girl in a loincloth hurried toward them from the trees beyond the shelter, carrying a spear and a basket. Her long reddish brown hair hid most of her face. "Josef!" she cried; he had taught her that much, at least. She scrambled toward them over the rocks, dropped the basket and spear at Josef's feet, then pulled at his arm.

Josef said, "She's jealous." The girl sat back on her heels and began to smooth her hair over her bare breasts. She lifted her head; her eyes were as black as Josef's. Orielna understood then what the girl was to him.

He had found his own eidolon in the Garden and would make her into his own image in time. He would deny her anything beyond his own needs, as Aniya had denied him his.

Josef got up and dragged the girl into the shelter. Orielna listened to their grunts and sighs as she gazed at the lake. Poor Josef, she thought; he thinks he's escaped Aniya, but he's only become what she would have been out here.

It was curious that she now felt so removed from everything around her. Her mind was probably becoming more unstable, since she was beginning to see why Josef welcomed his present state and embraced the wild and more violent impulses he saw as truly human. But she also pitied him. She might have become like him if she had come here alone, but knowing that she also had such impulses did not trouble her now. Uncertain as her fate was, she no longer feared it. Daro had shown her that she did not have to let mental shadows cloak her thoughts and deeds. Everything that had happened to her here was hers. She could become herself, then step beyond what she had been shaped to be.

She opened a channel. "Is Daro safe?" she whispered through it.

"He is," the Net replied inside her. "He freed himself without aid and touched us only long enough to say that his hunt was over. He is closed to us now. Do you wish us to assist you?"

The hunter had abandoned her, as Josef had guessed

that he might. Daro had, after all, only left her with the man she was seeking; he owed her no more than that. She should have expected it. He would go back to his hut to brood on his failure, perhaps leave the Garden altogether.

"I need no help," her thoughts whispered. "When Daro is open to you again, tell him that I won't forget him."

She closed herself off and bowed her head.

The girl struck a fire among the rocks and cooked the fish she had brought in her basket. Josef came out of the lean-to and studied Orielna for a moment. "You're just longing to summon help, aren't you?"

She blinked, holding back her tears. He would see only her unhappiness and not know that she had touched the Net. Her unfeigned sorrow, she supposed, was protecting her now; Josef was unaware of its cause. He could find out easily enough that she had disobeyed him if he opened a channel, but she no longer cared.

"The minds don't care what happens to you," he said, "or to anyone else. They'll look after us just to amuse themselves, but they don't care."

Orielna averted her eyes. Josef was wrong. The minds might have let their kind die out or overridden any troublesome or doubtful thought, but had not done so. Once, she had wondered why the Net allowed suffering that the minds could prevent. She realized now that the minds allowed them to choose what they would be, and surely there was some caring in that; they did not clutch at human beings as Aniya had clung to Josef, but left them free. The minds might think that there was hope for them then, that at least a few of them could choose more than their solipsistic dreams.

The girl pulled a fish from the fire and held it in front of her; Orielna recoiled. She seized Orielna's hair and forced her mouth against the fish while Josef laughed.

"Better eat," Josef said. "We don't have any other supplies." Orielna shook her head, afraid she might retch. The girl sat down, tore at the fish, gulped it down, picked her teeth with a few bones, then inched closer to Josef. Her hand slid toward one of the wands at his waist.

"Oh, no," he said gently, then slapped her, knocking her against the rocks. She wailed and covered her face.

"You don't have to treat her that way," Orielna said.

"It's all she understands." The firelight flickered across his face. He opened the front of his pants and threw himself at the girl, taking her on the rocks. Orielna watched them rut, then looked past them to the moonlit lake; there was no love in their act. Josef made no sound; she only knew that he had finished when he sat up and reached for more food. The girl adjusted her loincloth, then crawled toward him, draping her arms over his shoulders as she rested her head against his chest.

"You might be kinder to her," Orielna said.

"And do all the things I used to do for you and Aniya? I feel no need for that." He helped his companion up, then moved toward the lean-to. "Go to sleep."

She stretched out; her arms and legs ached from her bonds. Apparently Josef was not going to watch her, as she had expected. She waited until she could hear their even breathing, and wondered if he might be feigning sleep, waiting to see what she would do. A flyer could reach her before dawn if she asked for one, but Josef would hear it land, and she could not get to it bound as she was. She thought of his knife and how he might punish her for her disobedience.

She felt behind her, searching the smaller rocks with her

fingers, careful not to make a sound. The Moon was high when she finally found one with a sharp edge; she gripped it in her right hand and sawed at the leather strip around her left wrist. The leather was tough, her arms soon stiff from the effort; she rested, then hacked at the thong again. She had to get to the woods above the lake and summon help from there. Josef might come after her, though, and she had no way to defend herself. She could call for a flyer now, but she wasn't familiar enough with this region to know where in the forest it could land, or if she could find her way to it.

At last she felt the thong give way. Free, she rested for a bit, listening to the sounds of the sleepers, then sat up and untied the rope around her legs. Her arms and legs prickled; she rubbed at her ankles, wondering how soon she would be able to walk. A false step could send small rocks and pebbles down the beach and alert her captor. She steadied herself and got slowly to her feet.

Orielna crept toward the trees. She had nearly reached the edge of the forest when she heard his voice call her name. She spun around just in time to see Josef raise his wand; the beam shattered her thoughts and plunged her into a dark pool.

She was lost, lying on a hard, uneven surface, her back slightly arched, a weight against her abdomen. Her arms were out; someone held her down by the wrists. Orielna opened her eyes; the girl stood over her with one foot on Orielna's belly. Josef's face floated above her, his mouth where his eyes should be.

He said, "You shouldn't have done it." The black eyes below his mouth glistened. "You disappoint me. You've already called for aid, haven't you?"

"No," she managed to say. "I wanted to get away first."

"I'll find out if you're lying. It'll be a lot harder for you if you are. I didn't want to hurt you—I would have let you go if you'd behaved. You might have found that you didn't want to leave."

The girl's foot was heavier against her; she gasped from the pain, knowing that she had to open her link now. The girl suddenly turned her head. Orielna heard a sound that might have been a sharp gust of wind and then a queer thump.

Josef fell across her. The girl was screaming. Orielna struggled out from under Josef and sat up. The girl was running up toward the trees where Daro stood, her stone knife in her hand. A spear jutted from Josef's back. Orielna froze at the sight, then fumbled under him for a wand. Daro clutched a rock in his hand; the girl lifted an arm to hurl her knife. Orielna took aim; the beam shot into the girl's back. She fell and rolled slowly down the slope before coming up against a boulder.

The hunter scrambled toward her. She got to her feet as he caught her in his arms. "Are you all right?" he asked. "I was afraid I wouldn't reach you in time."

She leaned against him. "I didn't think you'd come. He told me not to open my link, but I had to know if you were safe. The minds said you'd given up, that you—"

"I had to leave him a false trail. He might have opened his own link."

She heard a groan and stepped back. "Josef," she murmured. Daro bent over him and pulled out the spear; blood gushed from the wound. The hunter knelt, tore a piece of cloth from one of his sleeves, and pressed it against Josef's back.

"He's healing now," he said. "Lucky it didn't kill him. If he'd left me my wand, I wouldn't have had to make a spear."

She straightened. The sun floated in the east above the

gray expanse of the lake. She could open her link now, but held back, wanting to feel this moment fully, both the wild joy and the terror of knowing she still lived.

"Your hunt was successful," she said at last. "You should leave a record of it all—others will probably admire your resourcefulness."

"Do you think that's the only reason I'm here?"

She moved toward him, afraid to hope. He was pleased that he had finished his hunt and that she was unharmed; had she been badly hurt, his success might have been tarnished. That was all his words could mean.

"What do you want to do with him?" he asked. "Take him back to his sharer? She might not want him now—she'd probably have him wiped."

"He would have preferred dying here to that," she said. "At least that death would have been his own."

"You decide." His mouth twisted as he looked up at her. "Aniya would expect it. Take him back, let her do what she likes with him, and then you can forget all of this."

"I don't know."

Josef stirred. Daro motioned toward the girl with his head. "You'd better watch her until she wakes up." He turned back to the wounded man.

When Josef was able to walk, Daro led him toward the shelter where Orielna sat, her wand aimed at the girl. The creature's dark eyes were wide as she glanced at the men; to her, it had to seem that her companion had risen from the dead. She would worship him all the more now.

Daro's spear and the girl's lay next to the lean-to; the other weapons, including the girl's knife, were tucked under the hunter's belt. He pulled out one of the wands as Josef sat down.

"What are you going to do?" Josef said. "Take me back? You might as well have me destroyed here. But you can't do that, can you? You have to let her decide."

Daro looked at Orielna. "She won't want me," Josef continued. "She'll hate what I've become. I'll have that satisfaction at least before I'm wiped."

Orielna said, "You're right. Aniya won't want you back now." She swallowed, repelled by Josef and the woman who had created him. "There's one way you can save yourself—all that matters is that others are safe from you. Open your link to the Net. The minds won't trouble your thoughts. As long as you stay here and they know where you are, you needn't be taken back. Any visitors can be warned to avoid you, and the Net can restrain you if you try to leave this place. This can be your prison."

Josef was silent.

"Aniya should be gratified," Orielna went on. "She'll believe that your thoughts might turn to her occasionally and that you'll regret this, but you'll have no way back to her if you do, and that will give her some satisfaction. If you find you can't bear your existence any longer, you can ask to be taken from here and destroyed. I think Aniya will agree to that."

"You think I'll choose to leave," he said, "now that you've told me this."

"No," she said, "you'll stay."

"Maybe the Net will override that decision."

She opened her link; the tendrils of her thoughts were caught in the web of minds. She felt their assent within herself; they had left the choice to them. She closed herself once more. "The minds won't override."

Josef pulled his lips back from his teeth. Daro picked up the spears as Orielna rose. "Don't think you can close your link completely," she said. "If you do, you'll only be hunted, and you won't get away next time."

"We'll leave your weapons up by the trees," Daro said. "You won't be able to go farther than that."

"Are you going back to her?" Josef asked. She turned away and began to climb the rocky slope, Daro at her side. "My link is open now. Wouldn't you like to have my thoughts flow into you one last time?"

She did not reply. "You surprise me," Daro murmured. "Can you leave him like that?"

"It's what he wants." Orielna looked back. The girl was following them, shaking her fist and muttering under her breath. Daro halted and raised his wand; the girl showed her teeth and then ran back to the shelter.

"That girl—" Orielna started to say.

"Let her live with the choice she made."

The girl hurried to Josef and embraced him. He knocked her away; Orielna heard her wild scream. She pawed at him; he grabbed her arm and pulled her into the shelter.

They came to a clearing and summoned a flyer to take them to Daro's hut. Orielna caught a glimpse of the lake on the horizon before the light, winged craft fled toward the sun over the treetops. Daro was silent, as he had been ever since they left the lake. Perhaps he was wondering just how much of Josef there was in her.

When the flyer landed, she climbed out after Daro. He glanced at her, a puzzled look on his face. "You're not leaving?" he said.

She shook her head. The craft lifted with a soft hum and flew toward the distant wall. "I hoped I could stay with you until I decide what to do."

"Until you decide." He drew his brows together. "Very well. I'll pitch a tent for myself."

"You don't have to—"

"Until you decide." He turned away.

The hunter spent the days listening to the minds or wandering along the creek without her. She passed her time alone, opening a channel occasionally to see if Aniya had called to her, but heard nothing.

A night came when she left the hut and went to Daro's tent. She heard him stir as she lifted the flap, afraid he might order her away, and then his arms were around her, drawing her to him. They moved slowly, lingering over each touch. She took her pleasure kneeling over him, then lay on her back, holding him tightly as he shuddered, sighed softly, and then was still.

"I want to stay here with you," she said. He stretched out next to her; she hooked one leg around his. "I want to listen to the minds with you and see if there are any unchanged people we might guide to the outside." She paused. "That is what you want to do, isn't it?"

"It'll be hard," he said, "finding ways to persuade them to come willingly, trying to show them they have nothing to fear—they might refuse us, even threaten us if we're too persistent. Even if we guide them through their change, we might fail in the end. They might decide to lose themselves among all those other hollow souls."

"That must be their choice," she said.

"And a painful and disappointing one for us if they make it. Or we might find that we can't give up enough of ourselves to join them if they decide to forgo our limits and become full partners of the Net."

She said, "I'll take the chance." His calloused hand slid

over her hip. "But I must do something else first. I have to see Aniya once more."

His hand stopped moving. "She knows what's happened here, and hasn't protested. There's no reason for you to see her."

"She's expecting me to come back. I have to tell her that I can't."

"You can do that from here," he said.

"I owe her more than that. I have to say it in her presence, so she knows it's over. Otherwise, she might keep hoping I'll come back, as she did with Josef."

He said, "You owe her nothing."

"Come with me, Daro."

He was silent for a long time. He would refuse, and she would have to go alone. "What is it, Orielna? Are you afraid to face her alone? Do I have to stand there thinking you might change your mind and stay, after all?"

"I won't stay. Please believe me—this is important. Come with me." She could not explain. She would know when he saw Aniya if he glimpsed anything of her in her sharer.

"Very well." He gripped her more tightly, as if he feared he might lose her.

They left the flyer and climbed the hill toward Aniya's house. The door opened as Orielna led Daro inside; they were expected. Aniya had said only that they could come, giving no sign of her feelings about the visit.

They were inside a bare, mirrored chamber. Orielna stared at the endless reflections of a slender, blond woman and a thickset, green-eyed man until the door leading to the courtyard opened.

Daro took her arm as they passed through the doorway.

Mats of various colors covered white tiles around a small pool; there were no plants, trees, or flowers. Orielna had passed many pleasant hours here with her sharer, but the courtyard now seemed stark and lifeless.

Aniya sat by the pool, her dark head resting on Karel's shoulder. The slim blond man glanced up at them with eyes as large and dark as Aniya's, then stroked his sharer's hair.

Aniya straightened and smoothed down her blue robe. Orielna searched the woman's fine-boned face for a sign of welcome, but Aniya's eyes were expressionless, her face stiff.

"So you've come back," Aniya said. Her gaze flickered over Daro; her mouth tightened. "I've been quite disoriented lately. Piro came here not long ago."

"Piro?" Orielna murmured, surprised.

"The lover I chose to forget."

"You mean the sharer you don't want to remember."

Aniya's head shot up. "Did he tell you? He had no right to do that."

"He didn't tell me," Orielna said. "Your secret is safely locked in the Net's records. Daro guessed it quite a while ago. I think I sensed he was right about that, even though I didn't realize it at the time."

"I'll have it wiped entirely," Aniya said in a sharper tone. "I won't remember him at all. He came here to remind me of what I was. He kept saying that he'd done me a great wrong, that he was like me once, that he left me in this house because he knew what I might do." She took a breath. "He thought I'd be safe here, protected from my impulses, the same ones he once had—he sounded quite unbalanced. He said he'd finally rid himself of the cruelty and fear he left in me, that he wanted me to come away with him and find out what I could be, that he wanted to make up for what he'd done. He said he'd found himself and that I could, too."

Orielna glanced at Daro. His face was filled with pity; he turned his head a bit toward her. His eyes grew warmer, and she knew then that he would not see Aniya when he looked at her.

"What a fool he was to come here," Aniya muttered. "He wanted me to remember it all again, but I won't."

"I came to tell you," Orielna said, "that I can't live with you anymore."

Aniya leaned forward. "Do you think I'd want you here now? You've grown much too different. I hoped you wouldn't, but I was prepared for that. I couldn't let you stay as you are, and there is Karel." The blond eidolon stroked her arm. "I'll wipe my mind of you, of Josef, of everything," she added in a strangely calm voice. "I won't retain any of it."

"And you'll go on being a shadow." Orielna lifted her arm. "Piro told you the truth about yourself. This place is your prison, but you can leave it. Release Karel and come away. Leave the trap you made for yourself."

"A trap?" Aniya smiled. "All finite life short of divinity is a trap, isn't it? We are God's forgotten eidolons." Her eyes went blank. Orielna opened her link slightly, then closed it again. Aniya had fled into a dream, perhaps one where her eidolons surrounded her, unchanged, gazing at her lovingly with her own eyes.

Karel got to his feet and said, "You've disturbed her enough."

"She might listen to you," Orielna said, knowing her words were futile. "Tell her she doesn't have to—"

Karel's lip curled. "You'd probably like to take her away and fill her with your own thoughts. She has what she wants, and so do I. My greatest joy comes when I link with her and know my thoughts are hers."

"I felt the same way once."

"You shouldn't have come here." Karel led them through the chamber of mirrors; the door slid open soundlessly. "I'm hers, and she's mine—I'll never want anything else. You could have been happy with us if you hadn't diverged, but maybe it's better this way. We can be everything to each other." There was a note of desperation in his voice; she wondered if he was aware of that.

A wind rippled the grassy plain below. Daro held her around the waist and kissed her gently on the forehead. "Did it hurt," he said, "when she told you she didn't want you here?"

"No." She gazed directly at him so that he would know that was true. They walked down the hill; she turned and looked back for a moment. Karel lingered by the entrance, then gazed out at the plain, as Josef used to do, before the door closed.

They passed through the gate and entered the wall's long evening shadow. A pavilion had been set up under the trees; a pale-haired woman in a violet shirt and pants sat under the canopy. A white cloth with a golden jug, a goblet, and a plate of pastries were spread on the ground in front of her.

"Greetings, Kitte," Orielna said as she and Daro approached.

Kitte nodded at them. "Please do sit down." She motioned with her wand. "There's plenty for all of us."

"I'm sure you didn't have it brought here so that you could welcome us back to the Garden."

"Not exactly." Kitte's violet eyes were calm, her perfect face composed. "Will you join me?"

Orielna glanced at Daro; he shrugged. "Very well," she replied.

"I'm afraid I have no other goblets," Kitte said, "but you're free to swig from the jug." Orielna and Daro seated themselves. "I didn't think you'd come back. Does this mean you've left your sharer?"

"She isn't my sharer now."

"No, I don't suppose she is. You've changed too much—even I can see that." Kitte handed the jug to the hunter. "You left my murderer in the Garden. That was his punishment—being allowed to stay where he wanted to be."

"It may be fitting," Daro said. "He chose it, and that may make it more of a punishment in the end."

"Well, it doesn't matter." Kitte smiled; she had the slightly unfocused look of someone with a completely open link. Orielna was relieved her own was closed, having no desire to glimpse any of this woman's thoughts. "He's alone now—did you know that? The Net verified it for me."

"Alone?" Orielna asked. Daro said nothing.

"Waiting for his unchanged girl. She hasn't come back for some time, and he's wondering where she is. Of course, he can't go to look for her."

Orielna frowned. "Maybe she went back to her people."

"She wouldn't go there," Daro said. "If she did, they'd see her as bewitched after being with a ghost so long. They'd drive her away."

"I suppose you'd know, being a hunter." Kitte's eyes narrowed as she studied Daro. "I thought myself that she might have another destination in mind, but I'm glad to hear you confirm that." She set down her goblet. "He must have believed she wouldn't dare to leave him."

Daro waved at the cloth and the tiny pastries. "Then this is a celebration of sorts."

"You might put it that way. He can feel a little of what I felt when he fled from me. He can wonder if some accident befell her, or if she finally grew to hate him." The woman sighed. "I am filled with suspense. I think I may wait here for a while."

"Perhaps you'd prefer to celebrate alone." Orielna stood up. "We must be going—we have quite a walk ahead of us."

Kitte waved her arm languidly. "Farewell."

Daro rose and followed Orielna from the pavilion. They had gone only a short distance before a rustling sound warned her that something was ahead. She took out her wand, listening to the sounds of panting and running footsteps.

The dark-eyed unchanged girl burst from the trees, snarling as she pushed past Orielna. Daro lifted his wand. The girl spun around, hissed, then slowly crept toward Kitte.

Orielna opened a channel. Josef's despairing wails echoed inside her, tearing at her mind; she muted them quickly. Daro caught her by the arm. She looked back long enough to see Kitte leading the girl toward the gate, then followed the hunter into the welcoming shadow of the forest.

The Renewal

1

As she gazed over the field, Josepha Ryba saw the maple tree. It dominated the clearing in front of her small house and marked the boundary between the trimmed lawn and the overgrown field. The tree was old, perhaps as old as she was. It had been there when she cleared the land and moved into her home.

The other trees, the hundreds along the creek in back of the house and the thousands on the slopes of the nearby hills, had to struggle. She and the gardeners had cleared away the deadwood and cut down dying trees many times. Gradually, she had become aware of changes. The pine trees across the creek flourished; the young oaks near the flat stones she had placed in a circle were gone.

Thirty paces from the maple a young apple tree grew. She had planted it a year ago—or was it two years? Two gardeners, directed by her computer, had planted the tree, holding it carefully in their pincerlike metal limbs. She did not know if it would survive. A low wire fence circled it to protect the tree from the small animals that would gnaw at its bark. The fence had been knocked over a few times.

Josepha looked past the clearing to the dirt road which wound through the wooded hills. A white hovercraft hugged the road, moving silently toward the field. The vehicle was a large insect with a clear bubble over its top. Small clouds of dust billowed around it as it moved. The craft stopped near the tangled bushes along the road, the bubble disappeared, and a man leaped gracefully out onto the road.

Merripen Allen had arrived a day late.

Josepha waved as he jogged toward her. He looked up and raised an arm. She wondered again why she had asked him to come. They had said everything and she had made her decision.

But she wanted to see him anyway. There was a difference between seeing someone in the flesh and using the holo, even if an image appeared as substantial as a body, at least until one reached out to it and clutched air.

He looked, as she expected, exactly like his image. His wavy black hair curled around his collar, framing his olive-skinned face. A thick moustache drooped around his mouth. But he seemed smaller than the amplified image, less imposing.

She was still holding her cigarette as he came up to her. She had been living alone too long and had forgotten how some felt about such filthy habits. She concealed it in her palm, hoping Merripen had not seen it, then dropped it, grinding it into the ground with her foot. She entered the house, motioning for him to follow.

Josepha disliked thinking about her life before the Transition. But her mind had become a network of involuntary associations, a mire of memories. She had been living in her isolated house for almost thirty years and would not have realized it without checking the dates. She had not believed it at first.

It was time to pack up and leave, go somewhere else, do something she had not tried. Her mind resonated here. The sight of an object would evoke a memory; an odor would be followed by the image of a past experience; an event, even viewed at a distance, would touch off a recollection until it seemed she could barely get through the day without succumbing to reveries.

Josepha was more than three hundred years old but she could still feel startled by the fact. She looked twenty-two—except that when she had actually been twenty-two she had been overweight, myopic, and had dyed her hair auburn. She had become, in what would have been her old age in another time, a slim woman with black hair and good vision. She was no longer plagued by asthma and migraine headaches and could not remember how they felt.

But she remembered other things. The events of her youth sprang into her mind, often in greater detail than more recent happenings. She had thought of clearing out the memories; RNA doses, some rest, and the reverberations would be gone, the world would be fresh and new. But that was too much like dying. Her memories made her life, uneventful and pacific as it was, more meaningful.

But now Merripen was here and the peace would soon end.

Merripen Allen slouched in the dark blue chair near the window. His dark brown eyes surveyed the room restlessly. He seemed weary, yet alert and decisive. All the biologists were like that, Josepha thought. They were the ones who had made the world, who kept it alive, who had banished death. They held the power no one else wanted.

Merripen was the descendant of English gypsies. His clipped speech was punctuated by his expressive arm gestures. Josepha suspected that he deliberately cultivated the contrast.

They had spent several minutes engaging in courtesies; exchanging compliments, describing the weather to each other, asking after people they each knew, making an elaborate ceremony of dialing for refreshments. Now they sat across the room from each other silently sipping their white wine.

Josepha wanted to speak but knew that would be rude; Merripen was still savoring the Chablis. He might want another glass and after that there would be more ceremonial banter, perhaps a flirtation. He would pay her compliments, embellishing them with quotations from Catullus, his trademark, and she would fence with him. She had gone through all this in abbreviated form with his image. A seduction, at least in theory, could last forever. Sex, however inventive, and however long it went on in all its permutations, grew duller. It was too much a reminder that other things still lived and died.

Merripen finished the wine, then gazed out her window at the clearing, twirling the glass in his fingers. At last he turned back to her.

"Delicious," he said. "Perhaps I'll have another." He rose to his feet. She motioned him to sit, got up, and walked slowly to the oak cabinet in the corner where the opened bottle stood. She brought it to him and poured the wine carefully, placed the bottle on the table under the window, then sat down again.

Merripen sipped. His visage blurred as she focused on the red rose in the slender silver vase on the low table in front of her. As she leaned back, the rose obscured Merripen's body. The redness dominated her vision; she saw a red bedspread over a double bed in the center of a yellow room. She was back in her old room, in the house of her parents, long ago.

She was fourteen and it was time to die. She locked her door.

The Renewal

She gazed at the small bottle, fumbling with the cap, suspended in time past, vividly conscious of the red capsules, the red bedspread, the cheerful flowered curtains over her window. The pain these sights usually brought receded for a moment. A voice called to her, the same soft voice that had called to her before, the disembodied voice she had never located.

She had been dying all along. The black void inside her had grown while the pain at its edges quivered. It would end now. As she swallowed the capsules, she was being captured by eternity, where she would live at last . . .

She had emerged from a coma bewildered, uncomprehending, connected to tubes and catheters, realizing dimly that she still breathed. She tried to cry out and heard only a sighing whistle. She reached with her left hand for her throat, touched the hollow at the base of her neck and felt an open hole. They had cut her open and forced her to live as they lived.

At night, as she lay in the hospital bed trying not to disturb the needle in her right wrist, she remembered a kind voice and its promise. Someone had spoken to her while she lay dying, while she hovered over her drugged body watching a tube forced into her failing lungs. The voice had not frightened her like the voice she had been hearing for months. It had been gentle, promising her that she would live on, that she would one day join it, and then had forced her to return. She was again trapped in her body.

Perhaps her illness or the barbiturates had induced the vision. Yet it had seemed too real for that. She knew dimly that she could not discuss it, could not make anyone understand it, could not even be sure it was real. She felt she had lost something without even being sure of what it was. But the promise remained: *not now, but another time.*

Josepha touched the rose and a petal fell. Her death was still denied her. She had lived, coming to believe she should not seek death actively, that three hundred, or a thousand, or a million years did not matter if the promise had been real.

Merripen spoke. She looked away from the rose.

The evening light bathed the room in a rosy glow. Merripen's skin was coppery and his tight white shirt was pinkish. "You are still with us," he said.

"Yes."

"You still want to be a parent to these children."

"Certainly." Josepha had decided to become a parent two years earlier and had registered her wish. Her request had been granted—few people were raising children now. Her genes would be analyzed and an ectogenetic chamber would be licensed for the fetus. She had been surprised when Merripen Allen contacted her, saying that before she went ahead with her plans he had a proposal to make.

He and a few other biologists wanted to create a new variant of humanity. They had been consulting for years, using computer minds to help them decide what sort of re-designed person might be viable. Painstakingly, they had constructed a model of such a being and its capacities, not wanting to alter the human form too radically for fear of the unknown consequences, yet seeking more than minor changes.

Merripen sighed, looking relieved. "I expected you wouldn't back out now, almost no one has, but two people changed their minds last week. When you asked me here I thought you had also."

She smiled and shook her head. It was Merripen's motives she wished to consider. She had worried that she might change her mind after seeing the child, but that was unlikely. There were no guarantees even with a normal child, since the biologists, afraid of too much tampering with human versatility, simply insured that flawed genes were not passed on rather than actively creating a certain type of child.

Even so, she had wondered when Merripen first made his offer. They had argued, he saying that human society was becoming stagnant while she countered by mentioning the diversity of human communities both on Earth and in space.

"We need new blood," he said now, apparently thinking along similar lines. "Oh, we have diversity, but it's all on the surface. I've seen a hundred different cultures and at bottom they're the same, a way of passing time. Even the death cults . . ."

She recoiled from the obscenity. "In Japan," he went on, "it's *seppuku* over any insult or failure, in India it's slow starvation and extreme asceticism, in England it's trial by combat, and here you play with guns. For every person we bring back from death, another dies, and the people we bring back try again or become murderers so that we're forced to allow them to die for the benefit of others." He glanced apologetically at her, apparently aware he was repeating old arguments.

Josepha did not want to think about death cults and the sudden flare-ups of violence that had reminded her of the Transition and had made her retreat to this house. She looked down at the small blue stone set into a gold bracelet on the Bond which linked everyone through a central system. The micro-computer link lit up and rang softly when someone called her; she could respond over her holo or touch her finger to the stone, indicating that she was unavailable and that a message should be left. More important, the Bond protected her and could summon aid. But even the blue stone could not guard her from everything; many knew how to circumvent the mechanism.

"But matters must be different in space," she replied, thinking of the huge, cylindrical dwellings that hovered in space at the Trojan points equidistant from Earth and Moon.

Merripen shrugged. "Not as much as you might think. The space dwellers were more innovative when they first left Earth, but now . . . you know, they pride themselves on being safe from the vicissitudes of life here, the storms, the quakes, the natural disasters. They make endless plans for space exploration and carry out none of them. Their cult is a cult of life with no risks."

"But there are the people on Mars, the ones out near Saturn, or the scientists who left our solar system a century ago. Surely they're not stagnating."

"They are so few, Josepha. And as for the ones who left, we have heard nothing. They may be dead or they may have found something, but in any event, it'll have no effect on us."

"I think you're too pessimistic," she argued, wanting to believe her own words. "How long have we had our extended lives? A little more than two hundred years. That's hardly long enough for a fair test. People change, they need time."

"I'm afraid the only thing time does for most people is to confirm them in their habits. Oh, some change, those who have cultivated flexibility. But they are so few. The others are a heavy weight holding us back. In the past, it took great deprivation and a strong leader to make such people change. There is no deprivation now and no leader. Perhaps these new children will open our eyes."

She found this turn in the conversation distasteful, but she had to expect such views from Merripen. He was too young to remember the surge of creativity, the high hopes that had existed for a short time after the difficulties of the Transition, but he knew of them and must sometimes long for them. She tried not to think of her own placid life and how hard it had been to force herself to consider being a parent. Stability, serenity, the eternal present—she would forsake them for something less sure. She thought of the ones who had left the solar system and wondered how they had brought themselves to do it.

"The children," she murmured. "I'd rather discuss them for a bit, settle some of my questions, I still don't understand completely." She was trying to draw Merripen away from his disturbing speculations.

"You've heard it all before."

"I didn't really listen, though. I didn't want to confront the details, I guess."

Merripen frowned. "If you're still ambivalent, you'd better back out now."

"But I'm not ambivalent. I agree with your general goal at least. And maybe part of it is that I'm afraid if I don't try something different now, I may never be able to . . . that's not the best motive, but . . ." She was silent.

"I understand."

"You said the children won't have our hormones. Won't that limit them?"

"That's not accurate," he replied. "Certain hormonal or glandular secretions are needed to insure their growth. But they won't be subject to something like the sudden rush of adrenaline we feel when disturbed or under stress."

"That could be dangerous. They might not react quickly enough."

"We've allowed for that. Refinements in the nervous system, quicker reflexes, will allow them to respond as quickly as we do, perhaps even a bit more quickly. The difference is that they won't act inappropriately. Our behavior is often the result of feelings, which are in turn rooted in our instincts and our survival biology. Their behavior will be based on rational decisions as much as on that."

"Our instincts have served us well enough in the past," Josepha murmured.

"They may not serve us well any longer. We don't have inevitable physical death anymore, yet our instincts probably go on preparing us for one. The rationality of these children will take the place of instinct and complement the instincts that remain."

Merripen paused as Josepha considered what he had told her before. The children would look human, but would have stronger muscles and bones less vulnerable to injury. They would have the ability to synthesize certain amino acids and vitamins, such as C and B_{12}; they would be able to live on a limited vegetable diet.

But the most extreme change, she knew, involved their gender. Merripen had explained that thoroughly, although she was aware that she had only a general understanding of it. They would have no gender—or maybe it was more appropriate to say they would have two genders. They would bear both male and female reproductive organs. They could reproduce naturally, each one able to be either father or mother, or by using the same techniques human beings now used. But they would lack sexuality. Their desires and ability to reproduce would become actualized only when they decided to have offspring; they would have conscious control of the process. Merripen had outlined this too in detail, but she recalled it only vaguely.

Josepha imagined that this radical alteration had probably alienated prospective parents who might otherwise have participated in the project. They must have thought it too much; sex had been separated from reproduction for ages and androgynous behavior was commonplace for men and women. Physically androgynous beings seemed unnecessary; the lack of sexuality, such a major part of human life, repellent.

Josepha was not bothered by it because sex, she thought sadly, thinking of the few men she had loved, had never been very important to her. But Merripen was reputed to be a compulsive sexual adventurer. She wondered if that was why he asserted that the children would be more rational without such an intense diversion. He might be fooling himself; the children might develop sexual desires of their own once they started to reproduce.

"We don't really know what they'll be like in the end," she said.

"We've done the projections," he answered. "We have a pretty good idea. But it *is* an experiment. Nothing is guaranteed." He picked up the empty wine bottle and turned it in his hands. "This entire society is an experiment. The results are not yet in. All of us crossed that line a long time ago."

The room had grown dark. Josepha reached over and touched the globular lamp on the table near her. It glowed, bathing the room in a soft blue light. "It's late," she said. "You're probably hungry."

He nodded.

"Let's have some supper."

Later, alone in her room, Josepha mused. She could not hear Merripen, who was in the bedroom at the end of the hall, but she sensed his presence. She had been alone in the house for so long that the presence of anyone impinged on her; her mind could no longer expand to fill up the house's empty space. She drew her coverlet over her.

Merripen had once discussed what he called the "natural selection" of immortality, his belief that certain mechanisms still operated, that those unsuited to extended life would fall by the wayside. He believed this even as he tried to prevent death. The Transition had weeded out many. The passing centuries would dispose of many more.

Ironically, she had survived. Nothing in her previous life had prepared her for this, yet here she was. She had been a student, a file clerk, a wife, a divorcée, a saleswoman, a sales manager, a wife again, a widow. She had been a passive graduate student who thought knowledge would give her a direction; she had succeeded only in gaining some small expertise on the pottery of Periclean Athens and in avoiding the real world. She had always worked because her first husband had been a student and her second an attorney paying child support and alimony to his first wife. Her purse had been snatched once, her home had been burglarized once, she had undergone two abortions. In this ordinary fashion, while the world lurched toward the greatest historical discontinuity it had ever experienced, Josepha had survived to witness the Transition. Only now did she feel, after so long, that she was even approaching an understanding of the world and her place in it.

She had been in her fifties when the techniques for extended life became available. The treatment had seemed simple enough; it consisted of shots which would remove the collagen formed by the cross-linkage of proteins and thus halt or retard the physical manifestations of aging. Even this technique, which could make one no younger but only keep one from aging as rapidly, had created controversy, raising the specter of millions of old citizens lingering past their time. Many chose to die anyway. Others had themselves frozen cryonically after death, hoping they would be revived when medical science could heal them and make them live forever. Cryonics became big business. Some concerns were legitimate. Many were fraudulent, consigning their customers to an expensive, cold, permanent death.

Josepha, retired but in need of extra money, became a maintenance worker for a cryonic interment service. She walked among the stacks of frozen dead, peering at dials. By chance, she found that several of her fellow workers dealt illegally in anticollagen shots, selling them to people under the mandatory age of sixty-five for recipients. Knowing that penalties for selling the shots were severe, she was too frightened to become a pusher. But she bought a few shots.

Soon after, work on the mechanisms which caused cancers to multiply, along with genetic research, had yielded a way of restoring youth. Research papers had been presented tentatively; most people had waited cautiously, until at last impatience outran caution and the world entered the Transition in bits and pieces, one country after another.

There were failures, although few wanted to remember them now; people who were victims of virulent cancers, those who could not be made younger, a few who grew younger and then died suddenly. Some theorized that the mechanisms of death could not be held in check forever; that in the future, death might come rapidly and wipe out millions. Testing the new technique thoroughly would have taken hundreds of years, and people would not go on living and dying while potential immortals were being sustained in their midst.

Everyone knew about the Transition, the upheavals, the collapsing governments, the deaths, the demands. There were some facts not fully known, that were still strangely absent from computer banks and information centers; exact figures on suicides, records of how many were killed by the treatments themselves, who the first subjects had been and what had happened to them. Josepha had searched, and found only unpleasant hints; one small town with a thirty percent mortality rate after treatment, prisoner-subjects who had mysteriously disappeared, an increase in "accidental" deaths. She had lived through it, surviving a bullet wound as a bystander at a demonstration of older citizens, hiding out in a small out-of-the-way village, and yet any present-day historian knew more than she could remember. She suspected that the only people who knew almost everything were a few old biologists and any political leaders who were still alive.

In her nineties, half-blinded by cataracts, hands distorted into claws by arthritis, Josepha had at last been treated and begun her extended life. She had survived Peter Beaulieu, her first husband, and Gene Kolodny, her second. She had outlived her brother and her parents and her few close friends. And until now, she often thought, she had done little to justify that survival.

She could not accept that so many had died for the world as it was now. The vigor and liveliness had gone out of human life, or so it seemed. Perhaps those who would have provided it were gone and the meek had inherited the Earth after all.

But she could change. She was changing. Either the death cultists were right and their lives were meaningless or their extended lives were an opportunity which must be seized. She recalled her own near-death and the promise of

The Renewal

another life; even that possibility did not change things. She had to earn that life, if there was such a thing, with a meaningful life here, and if there was no other life, then this one was all she had.

More than three hundred years to discover that—it was absurd. There were no more excuses for failure, which explained the suicides and death cults at least in part. Merripen's project would force the issue. She remembered how his enthusiasm for his dream had been conveyed to her during their first discussion, in spite of her doubts. She thought: maybe most of us are slow learners, that's all, well, we'll learn or be supplanted.

She refused to think of another possibility; that the world might not accept the children, that any future beyond the present was unthinkable.

Josepha arrived at the village where the parents and children were to live a month after her visit with Merripen. Three houses, resembling chalets, stood on one side of a clearing. Four others, with enclosed front porches, sat almost two hundred meters away on the other side of the clearing. Behind them, on a hill, she saw a red brick structure which was large enough for several people.

A bulldozer, a heavy lumbering metallic beast, excavated land doggedly while two men watched. She assumed that the two were involved in the project, although they might be only curious bystanders.

Josepha walked through the clearing, which would be transformed into a park. A tall African man stood on the porch of one house, his back to her. She saw no one else. She came to a stone path and followed it, passing the unoccupied houses. Each was surrounded by a plot of ground which would become a garden. The park would eventually contain two large buildings; a hall where everyone could gather for meals, recreation, or meetings, and a hostel for the children. One part of the recreation hall would be used as a school.

The path ended at a low stone wall. Josepha stood in front of an open metal gate and looked past a small courtyard at a two-story stone house. She approached the gray structure and peered through a window. She saw sturdy walls instead of movable panels, a stairway instead of a ramp, and decided this was where she would live. The house was too large for only one parent and child, but she could find someone to share it with her.

She heard footsteps and turned. The tall African man stood at the gate. He adjusted his gold-trimmed blue robe and bowed slightly. She returned the bow and moved toward him, stopping about half a meter away. His black hair was short and his beard closely trimmed. "Chane Maggio," he said in a deep voice as he extended his right hand.

She was puzzled, startled by the lack of ceremony. She suddenly realized that he was telling her his name. He continued to hold out his hand and at last she took it, shook hands, and released it. "I'm Josepha Ryba."

"You are startled by my informality." He folded his slender arms over his chest. "Perhaps I am being rude, but we have little time to become acquainted, only a few months before gestation begins and then only nine months to the birth of the children. I am afraid we cannot stand on ceremony in our salutations."

She smiled. "How long have you been here?"

"I arrived this morning. I believe we are the only prospective parents here." He offered his arm and she took it. They began to amble along the stone path.

She sensed that Chane Maggio remembered the Transition. She was not sure how she knew; perhaps it was the informality of his greeting, the sense of contingency in his voice, or his silence now as they strolled. Younger people always wanted to fill the silences with words or games or actions of some kind. The Transition was only history to them. To Josepha, and those like herself, it would forever be the most important time of their lives, however long they lived. It had made them survivors with the guilt of survivors. The simplest sensation meant both more and less to them than to those born later. Josepha, acutely conscious of Chane's arm, the clatter of their sandals on the stones, the warm breeze which brushed her hair, remembered that she was alive and that others were not and that she was somehow coarsened by this. A younger person, caught in the timeless present, would accept the sensations for themselves.

"This venture promises to be most interesting," Chane said softly in his deep voice. "I have raised children before—I had a son and daughter long ago—a rewarding task, watching a child grow, trying to—" He paused.

Josepha waited, not wanting to be rude by interrupting. "There are problems, of course," he continued, and she caught an undercurrent of bitterness and disappointment. "There is always the unexpected." His voice changed again, becoming lighter and more casual. "They live on Asgard now, at least they did fifty years ago. They claim it's too dangerous to live here."

"I once wanted to visit a space community," Josepha said. "For years I kept intending to go, but I never did."

"More people live in space than on Earth, but of course you know that."

"I didn't know."

Chane raised an eyebrow. "I was a statistician for many

years. There are approximately two billion people on Earth and almost twice as many in space."

"That many," Josepha murmured, inwardly chastising herself for not knowing. She could have asked her Bond.

"Of course, there has been a small but noticeable decline in the population." The man paused again, having strayed too near an unpleasant topic. "Tell me," he went on, "did you ever make pottery? I believe I own a vase you made, it was a gift from a friend."

"That was a long time ago. I had a shop with a friend, Hisa Onoda. Hisa made jewelry and I did pottery, that was a little while after the Transition, when we all still had to credit purchases to our accounts."

"This was later, after accounts."

"Well, we stayed in business after that just for our amusement. We'd trade our items for things we liked, paintings, sculptures, but the Whatfor finally ruined it for us. We refused to duplicate anything we made, but others duped the items anyway."

"Even so," he said, "what is important about a thing is its beauty or utility, not its scarcity."

"I know that," she replied. "I don't think Hisa understood it, though. She'd always made jewelry, things like that. It was important to her that each item be unique, she used to tell me that everything she made was only for a certain individual, was right for that person and wrong for anyone else. Sometimes she would refuse to sell a particular object to a customer, she would insist that he look at something else. What's strange is that the customer would always like the item she would pick out more." An image of Hisa's small body crossed her mind: Hisa in her sunken tub, wrists slashed, lips pale, red blood in swirls on the water, her Bond detached and resting helplessly on the floor. *Too late.*

Josepha quickly buried the image. "I'd been a salesperson before the Transition, but Hisa made it an art."

"I was a politician," Chane said. He stopped walking and released her arm. "Does that startle you?"

She thought: what must you have done? She did not reply; she could not judge him.

"I was fortunate. I survived because I saw clearly where things were going and knew when to relinquish my power and wait. I saw that those in power could not hold the tide back indefinitely, and that those who tried to hang on would suffer—as they did."

She listened, only too conscious of her own past sins of omission. She had heard the stories of powerful people who had gained access to the treatments, then given up their positions to go into hiding. Not all had survived. Others had kept their power, many hoping to restrict the gift of extended life to themselves. Both groups bore responsibility for the collapse of civil order at the beginning of the Transition.

"I have changed," he was saying. "I have little interest in such things now." She nodded, almost hearing his unspoken challenge: would it be better if I had died?

The mood of their meeting had been destroyed. Chane bowed, murmured a few courteous phrases, and departed.

The other parents had arrived, one at a time, for the past few months. Construction was finished; the machines had moved to a nearby lake, where three lodges would be built.

Josepha, unused to groups, had grown more reticent. She was quiet at the frequent parties for the thirty prospective parents and at the meetings with the biologists and psychologists who lived nearby. The parties were usually formal; word games were played, objects and sensations were exhaustively described or put into short poems in various languages by the literarily gifted. Direct questions were never asked.

Most of the villagers had remained only names to her. She saw Chane Maggio fairly often, although even he seemed more reserved. Wanting to know more about her companions, she had resorted to the public records in her computer.

She had discovered what she had suspected; most of them were veterans of the Transition. Had Merripen wanted older people, or were older people the only ones willing to volunteer for the project?

Her other discoveries were more intimidating. She reviewed them now as she sat in her living room knitting a sleeve for a sweater. The villagers included Amarisa Drew, who had been both an agronomist and a well-known athlete, Dawud al-Ahmad, former poet and chief engineer of the Asgard life support systems, and Chen Li Hua, a clothing designer and geologist.

She looked up from the blue wool and saw Merripen Allen entering her courtyard. She called to him, telling him to enter. Her door slid open; Merripen stamped his feet in the small foyer, then entered the living room.

He settled in a high-backed gray chair in the corner across from her. "What can I do for you?" she asked.

"I've been visiting each person here individually, I want to be sure there aren't any problems and that everybody's settling in. I hope you'll all start loosening up soon, get to know each other better."

"That takes time," she said, "especially if you're used to solitude. And I have to . . ."

"Yes?"

"I don't quite know how to put it. Everyone else seems so accomplished."

The Renewal

"It's difficult to live a long time without that being the case."

"No it's not," she replied. "I haven't done much."

Merripen chuckled. "Almost everyone I've seen has told me that. So I'll have to tell you what I told them. First of all, I wouldn't have asked any of you to become involved unless I had a good opinion of you. Second, although I've always admired modesty, I don't like meekness, especially in prospective parents who need strength for any problems they may face. You should all be more at ease when you become better acquainted."

"I guess," she responded, as if accepting his exhortation. He was not deceiving her. Almost no one wanted to be a parent now; of the few who did, most had probably rejected Merripen's offer. He had probably taken those he could get, rejecting only those obviously unsuitable.

Merripen seemed worried. He was pulling at his moustache. Josepha resumed her knitting. "I hope," she said, "that you're not having doubts." She said it lightly.

"Of course I am," he replied, startling her with his harsh tone.

"But then why—"

"Not about you people, not about whether we should go ahead, that's settled." She sat up stiffly, clutching her needles, shocked at the way he had interrupted her in midsentence.

"I'm terribly sorry, please forgive me," he said more quietly. "At any rate, I didn't come here to discuss my worries. I wanted to talk about your child. Have you decided on who the second parent will be, or do you intend to form a liaison with one of the people here?" Each child, she knew, was to have two parents, as that would provide each with more links to other human beings and avoid possible emotional problems for a parent whose child was his or hers alone. It was hoped that the children would regard all of the people in the village as members of a family. "We need time to make tests, as you know," he went on. "We have to check for possible incompatibilities or flaws that need correcting."

"I've decided. I made up my mind a while ago and just didn't realize it till now." She put the knitting aside. "Nicholas Krol."

"Excuse me?"

"Nicholas Krol," she repeated. "The other parent. He was a composer, maybe you've heard the name."

"Did you know him?"

"Yes, I knew him, I knew him well. I was in love with him." As she spoke, Josepha saw Nicholas Krol's steady gray eyes and his ash brown hair, but she could not remember his face clearly. Something inside her seemed to break at the realization. "I met him after my divorce, we lived together for a couple of years. He was ambitious, he wanted me to be ambitious too, accomplish something, but I was afraid to try, too afraid of failing. We broke up finally, he didn't want to, but I—" For a moment, she recalled his face. She tried desperately to hold it in her mind, and lost it.

"Why?" Merripen asked. "Why Krol?"

"I don't know if I can explain it. He challenged me, he encouraged me. Everyone else just accepted me the way I was. I shouldn't have left him."

"Then why did you leave?"

"Because it was easier to give up."

Merripen seemed puzzled. "It seems a strange motive for picking him, your having regrets."

"It isn't only regrets. He was the most important person in my life, although it took me much too long to see that."

She realized she sounded shrill. "I was self-destructive when I was in my twenties, always acting against my own self-interest. That's why I left Nick. Later I changed, and acquired a sort of stubborn passivity." She closed her eyes for a moment, waiting for her sorrow and bitterness to pass.

"May I be frank?" the biologist asked. She nodded. "You want the child of a man you loved long ago, so perhaps you're trying to recapture that love. Is Krol still alive?"

She shook her head.

"So guilt enters the picture as well. You're alive and he isn't. Do you even know whether we can acquire his genetic material?"

"He would have had his sperm frozen, I know it. You don't know what he was like. He would have made sure of it. He had a bit of vanity, I used to tease him about it."

"I'm sorry, Josepha. I think you're making a mistake."

"If you have another suggestion, please offer it. I'm willing to listen. But I don't think I'll change my mind."

"I would like your child to be mine as well."

She stiffened in surprise. She was sure that the man had no romantic interest in her. "Why?"

"I'm in charge of this project, it was really my idea in the beginning. I'll be living here most of the time, it seems only suitable that I should also be a parent and share this role with you people. If you wish, I can become your lover, if you feel that would strengthen our bond as parents."

The proposal repelled her. She picked up her knitting. Her needles clicked. She heard a few Chinese phrases as two people passed the gate outside. At last she put down the needles and looked at Merripen.

"I must say no." She could not leave it at that. "I think it would be a mistake for you to have your own child here. If you're going to be in charge, you shouldn't be in a position where you might favor one child over the others. And you should try to preserve some objectivity."

"You think it's possible for anyone to be completely objective?"

"Of course not. I do think you can get so personally involved that you don't notice certain things, that emotional considerations become more important. And anyway, I think you want this child out of some misplaced desire to be like all of us here—you can feel noble, not asking us to do something you wouldn't do yourself, and . . ." She paused. "There's only one reason for having a child, Merripen."

"And what is that?"

"Because you want to help another human being learn and grow. You should regard all the children here as yours. Isn't that enough for you? You don't have to prove anything to the parents here, and you might ruin what you're working for by trying."

"You won't reconsider?"

"No. I suppose, if you wanted to, you could prevent me from having a child at all as well as barring me from the project."

"What do you think I am?" Merripen replied in injured tones. "We don't force our desires on others, our work is for everyone's benefit. You should know that by now."

"You have power whether you want it or not and whether you want to recognize it or not. Everyone knows it. It's just nicer not to mention it."

"Are my wishes more irrational than yours?" He smiled lopsidedly. "You want a dead lover as the father."

"I knew him. Krol's child will have intelligence and strength. And if we really do value life as much as we profess to, then what is so irrational about wanting some part of a dead man to live again?"

He slouched in his chair. For a moment, Josepha thought she saw conflicting emotions in his dark eyes, disappointment warring with relief. He had made his noble gesture without having to follow it up.

"You have to remember," the biologist said softly, "that these children will not be quite like us. You may be disappointed if you're trying to recapture something you've lost."

Josepha sighed. "I suppose you'll ask someone else to be a parent with you."

"No. The others have already made their choices."

She felt relieved by the answer, but remained disturbed. She worried again about Merripen's reasons for beginning the project.

Josepha had gradually become better acquainted with the other village residents. She felt most at ease with the three now sitting at her round mahogany table sipping brandy; Vladislav Pascal, a small, wiry man who had been a painter, Warner Chavez, a tall, slender woman with impossibly large black eyes who was once an architect, and Chane Maggio.

Warner and Vladislav were going to raise a child together. Many of the villagers had already paired off or formed groups, but Josepha was still alone.

She had gone that afternoon to the nearby laboratory where the embryos were gestating. She had peered at the glassy womb enclosing her child, Krol's child—it had looked like all the others. Feeling vaguely uneasy, she had left quickly.

Looking around the table at her guests, Josepha saw Warner gaze sleepily at Vladislav. Chane had said little all evening as the three reminisced about their second youth, during the Transition, everyone's favorite topic lately; even the hardships of the period had acquired a benign glow in retrospect. The shabbiness of the towns and decay of the cities had not mattered to any of them. With their newly youthful bodies and restored health, anything had seemed possible.

Josepha had migrated to the nearest large city after her treatments, with hordes of others. She had lived in a decrepit hotel, sharing a bathroom with ten people and had not minded. Surrounded by people constantly meeting to plan new cities, new machines, new arts, new ventures and experiments, she had known that the hardships would be temporary. They were all high on dreams, sure the worst was over, too busy to remember the dead. Now she sat, like the others, amid what they had built and looked backward to the building and dreaming while awaiting a new beginning.

Warner smoothed back her thick red hair and rose. Vladislav got up also. "No, don't show us out," he said to Josepha before she could stand. "Lovely meal, lovely. Don't forget tomorrow, we're expecting you both. Most of the village will probably be there and we'll all try to forget that it's a party for the psychologists." He bowed to Chane and the couple left.

Chane seemed abstracted. He toyed with his snifter. She said nothing, sensing that he wanted silence.

She did not know Chane that well in spite of his frequent visits. The public record of his life had told her little. He had been his African nation's ambassador to China, then its foreign minister during the years before the Transition. His grandfather had been an Italian. His life during the Transition was a mystery. But somehow she was at ease with him. She could sit there pursuing her own thoughts while he was lost in his own. Occasionally they looked at each other and

The Renewal

smiled; they did not have to fill the silences with words.

Tonight he seemed more apprehensive than usual. She lit a cigarette and pushed the ivory cigarette box to him across the table; Chane too was a secret smoker. He shook his head. "I must ask you something, Josepha. I've been putting it off. May I be open with you?" His deep voice was subdued.

"Of course."

He put his hands in front of him, palms down on the dark wood. "I must tell you something first. As you know, I was married in my previous life and had a family. You have undoubtedly guessed that my relations with them left something to be desired."

She nodded, not knowing what to say.

"My wife was an intelligent, educated woman and I thought enough of her to make her one of my advisors. We married late in life, in our thirties. We agreed on everything, almost never fighting. After our children were born, I began to feel that she became more demanding, that instead of helping me, she was distracting me. I began to blame her for everything that went wrong. Eventually, I took to spending more time away from her. It probably seems a familiar story. Eventually, we separated. I was very bitter about it."

"Chane, why are you telling me this? You don't have to justify yourself to me, I made plenty of mistakes too."

"But I want you to understand this before I make my request. It took a long time for me to see that much of this was my fault. I was telling myself how important my ministry was, my country was in a very difficult period then and I couldn't take the time for personal problems."

"Wasn't it true?"

"Of course it was," he replied. "It's no excuse. Work is a

wonderful thing, especially demanding work. It means you have a good excuse for not trying to solve your personal problems, for avoiding them, for taking and not giving because the work is more important than anything."

"Well, sometimes it is, isn't it?" She stubbed out her cigarette, spilling some ashes on the table.

"Oh, sometimes. Very rarely. The world is moved by historical forces, by certain developments, by things we don't control."

"The Transition changed things, and that was the result of scientific research by a few people."

Chane finished his brandy and lit a cigarette. "A transition of some sort was bound to happen anyway, events were moving toward one. It was a more complex situation than you imply. The world was already changing and the biologists only hastened it. Look at them now. What can they really do?"

Josepha shook her head. "You're wrong, Chane. Here we are with this project. You're saying it won't make any difference at all, but you're here just the same. You're contradicting—"

"No, you don't hear what I'm saying." His voice was firm. "There is only one way people can influence the future and that is by the quality of their relationships with others, the ways in which they treat people, caring about them and showing it constructively. Sharing what you might learn with someone, loving someone, raising a child to be both inquisitive and compassionate. There is no one more powerless than a person who has the power to intervene, you either become driven by it and by forces you don't understand, holding it at whatever cost, or you realize that all you can do is be a moral and rational example, a symbol perhaps of something better. Or you run away in the end, as I did."

Chane paused. A pale blue wisp of smoke circled his head. "Merripen believes," he continued, "that the children here will change the world, in other words, that he himself will. It's a deception. Yes, they may make a difference, but not because of a peculiar physiological makeup. It will be our relationships with them as parents, our personal attention, how we act toward them, that will make them what they might be. If we raised a group of children like ourselves and tried to give them a creative and open view, the results might very well be similar. Except that it may be easier for these children."

"Yet you agreed."

He smiled. "Oh, yes. I wanted to be part of it, I don't want to run away as I did before."

Josepha considered Chane's arguments. She was not sure that she agreed; it seemed that the combination of heredity and environment was needed. But she did not feel like arguing about it now. "Who is to be your child's other parent?" she asked.

"My wife, of course. You're surprised. She's still alive and she agreed. I've been lucky, able to patch things up instead of living with guilt and ghosts." The statement seemed forced. Josepha looked down as he spoke. "She's a stranger now," he went on. "I suppose I am too."

"What did you want to ask me before, Chane?"

"I . . . it's hard to know how to phrase it. I'd like you to consider sharing your life here with me, raising our children together."

She looked up, startled. He lowered his eyes and put out his cigarette. She knew that she found Chane attractive, although neither of them had nourished the attraction with the usual romantic games and ploys. She liked him. It seemed a rather weak foundation for a relationship.

"Why?" she asked gently.

"I feel at ease with you, that's the main reason. Let's try it at least, if it doesn't work out I can move again after the children are born." Something in the tone of his voice reminded her of Merripen Allen. Again, she worried about the reasons for the project. She thought: it's a mistake, it may hurt the children in the end, it will change all of us here forever.

But that was false. If it failed, it would change nothing and would be forgotten by the parents as everything was when one had enough time. She shook her head.

"You're refusing me, then," Chane said.

"Oh, no, I was thinking of something else. I'd like you to stay, this house is really too big for one parent and child." That sounded too cold, too pragmatic. "I think we'll get along," she added.

She wished that she could feel happier about the decision.

Josepha adjusted easily to Chane's presence. Their life together was marred only by an occasional gentle argument. But Chane remained impenetrable. Josepha imagined that she must appear the same way to him. Even their lovemaking did not bridge the gap.

It was probably just as well, she thought. This way, at least, she could preserve some sense of privacy. Both could keep an emotional equilibrium that would conserve their strength, the strength they would need when the children were born.

She knew, however, that they could not remain on that peaceful plateau forever. Their shared lives would force them into confrontations sooner or later. But it was hard to break old habits, difficult to believe that there might not be time enough to let events happen and allow differences to be resolved. Better, she knew, to settle each issue as it came up, instead of trying to sort everything out now.

When she finally realized that there had been no time, only a few months, and that she and Chane were still far from understanding very much about each other, all the children were ready to leave their wombs and enter her world.

2

Teno, her child, Krol's child, was with her at last. Teno had no surname; it was customary to let people choose their own last names.

She had been surprised at how ordinary, how normal, the child appeared. Teno had her dark hair, a face like a small bulldog, and olive skin. She could see nothing of Nicholas Krol in the child; perhaps that resemblance would come with maturity.

Josepha often felt tired. She leaned against the courtyard gate, inhaling the mild spring air, grateful for a few moments to herself. The flow of time had fragmented into a million discrete segments which seemed to jostle against each other. The children had to be fed, washed, taken outside for a few minutes of air, played with, hugged, dressed, undressed, and put to bed. The village had shaken off its lassitude; the children were now the center of everything. It would have been easier to let the psychologists, with the aid of a few robots, assume many of the parental duties, but almost no one took much advantage of that. It was as if they all wanted to be sure nothing went wrong, that the children would not be damaged by neglect.

"Hey!" a woman's voice shouted. Warner Chavez was approaching her along the stone path. Josepha put a finger to her lips as she opened the gate.

"Everyone's asleep," she exclaimed as her friend entered the courtyard. "Even Chane, he's exhausted. He was up at dawn with Teno and Ramli." Ramli was Chane's child.

Warner smiled. "So's Vlad, he and Nenum are probably both stacking deltas by now." Josepha found herself thinking: men don't have as much stamina. She was mildly ashamed of the thought.

Warner sat down on the grass, folding her trousered legs in a half lotus. There were pale blue shadows under her black eyes. Josepha sat down with her back against the stone wall, wrapping her arms around her legs. She too was tired, not fatigued enough to sleep, but too weary to concentrate. A part of her always seemed removed, watchful, listening in case the children should need her. Chane was like that too. Neither of them could sit for more than a few minutes lately without listening for sounds or getting up now and then to check things.

Warner was gazing at the red tulips blooming in a row next to the house. She looked away quickly, probably wondering why Josepha planted such short-lived flowers. "Tell me, Jo, have you talked to Chane much about the children?"

Josepha shrugged. "We haven't had that many conversations lately. It's hard to keep talking when you're tired all the time, I can't even watch the holo without feeling sleepy. I guess I didn't think looking after them would take so much out of me."

"What I meant was, has Chane said anything to you about the kids. He was a parent once, wasn't he?"

The Renewal

"What do you expect him to say about them?"

"What they're like compared to normal . . . compared to other kids. Maybe I'm being silly, but there's something unnerving about them."

"Is there?" Josepha rested her chin on her knees. "Teno's really not much of a problem, all things considered. I was expecting all kinds of little crises."

"Think about the way they cry, for instance. Doesn't it seem strange to you?"

"Is it strange?" Josepha asked. "I wouldn't know, I suppose, I was never around children that much. My brother Charlie was older than I was, and I didn't have a younger brother or sister."

"Well," Warner replied, "it's not that awful squalling I remember, the kind of crying that sounds like a cat in heat and you know the poor kid is colicky or damp or maybe hungry. With these kids, it's more of a steady cry, I don't know how to describe it. It's . . . calm, steady and calm. Sometimes I'll hear a real howl, but it's as if they're only exercising their lungs. That's what my Nenum does anyway, and others too. Aren't Teno and Ramli like that?"

Josepha nodded. "That isn't normal?"

"No." A breeze ruffled Warner's long red hair. "All right, they're not quite like us, with their immunities and their modified neurons and reflexes, they weren't meant to be, but they look so much like ordinary kids that . . . I picked up Nenum yesterday, after a nap, just to hug my child, you know the feeling. You just want to let them know you're there and you care. Nenum just sort of put up with it, that's all. It's always like that. I can't describe it any other way. There's just no response at all."

"Maybe you're making too much of it, Warner. You said it yourself, they weren't meant to be like us, that's the point of the project. Anyway, things don't look right when you're tired most of the time, you make more of them or think something's the matter when it isn't."

"I know that."

"They're still our children."

"Of course. They made sure of that, genetic bonds as well as emotional ones." Warner's fine-featured face contorted. "I don't know what they'll be. I don't know what they are or what they'll become. I don't even know whether Nenum is my son or daughter, am I supposed to call my child 'it'?" Her slender body drooped.

"Does that really matter? It wouldn't change how you act toward Nenum. And you didn't know what your other children would be like, or what kinds of adults they would become."

"I knew they were human," her friend said harshly. "I can't even look at Nenum without remembering that, I keep seeing . . . maybe I wasn't ready for this, Jo."

Josepha felt at a loss. She tried to look reassuringly at Warner. "Yes, you were," she said as firmly as possible. She got up and sat near her friend, putting an arm over the red-haired woman's shoulders. "Look, Merripen wouldn't have had you come here if he thought otherwise." She tried to sound convincing, recalling her doubts about how Merripen had selected the parents. "It's normal to have doubts. Maybe when you feel this way you should just go and hold Nenum and put those thoughts out of your mind. It doesn't matter. You and Vladislav have to take care of your child, that's all. Think of things that way."

Warner smoothed back her hair with the chubby hands that seemed unmatched to her slim arms. "You're right. Maybe I'm just disoriented. I'm not used to anything different after all this time."

The Renewal

Josepha, hearing a cry, suddenly sat up. The cry was steady, punctuated by short stops, a smooth cry without any variation in pitch. A second cry, slightly lower, joined the first. Teno and Ramli were awake.

Teno and Ramli were toddlers, trying to walk.

Only a short time ago, it seemed, the children had been unable to sit up. Now Josepha and Chane watched as the two struggled across the floor.

She and Chane had preserved their quiet and reserved relationship. Much of their conversation concerned the children. Their lovemaking was partly a formality, partly a friendly and often humorous way of reassuring each other during moments of loneliness. Most of the time it was easier for each of them to wire up and live out a fantasy encounter.

Chane sat at one end of the sofa, Josepha at another. Ramli toddled unsteadily toward Chane and stretched out small brown hands to him. Teno moved to Josepha, grabbing for her arms almost before she held them out.

"Very good!" she said brightly. Teno, solemn-faced, held her hands for a moment, then sat on the floor. Chane picked up Ramli, seating the baby on his lap. He held up a hand, holding out one finger, and Ramli began to pull at the other fingers Chane had concealed. The child studied them intently for a moment, then quietly looked away, as if losing interest.

The children were always like that. If she or Chane wanted to play a game, they would respond in a serious, quiet way. If she wanted to show them some affection, they put up with it, with expressions that almost seemed to say: I can do without this, but obviously you need it.

What did they need? She watched as Chane placed

Ramli on the floor. The two children crawled over the rug, peering intently at its gold and blue pattern. Did they require something they were not receiving from the adults around them? An observant person could tell if an ordinary child might be having a serious problem. Even given the wide variations in normal behavior, abnormal responses became obvious in time. But they did not know what normal behavior would be for these children.

She sighed, thinking of old stories; children raised by wolves who could never learn to speak, could never really be human. She watched as Teno and Ramli poked at the bright spot where a beam of sunlight struck the rug.

Teno looked like her, with black hair, olive skin, high cheekbones—but the eyes were not her brown ones. One could look at dark eyes and read expressions too easily. Knowing this, Josepha had always had difficulty gazing directly at people, wondering if they could read her thoughts. Teno's eyes were Krol's gray ones, impossible to read, always distant. She saw the quiet, mildly curious expression on her child's face and was suddenly frightened.

But that was foolish. She had been listening to Warner too often. She must stop giving credence to Warner's recurring doubts and worrisome hypotheses.

She realized that Chane was staring at her. Her worries must be showing on her face. She smiled reassuringly. His sad eyes met hers; he did not smile back. Then he turned his head toward the window.

She felt like reaching out to him, holding him, and the force of her desire surprised her. But she restrained herself, and the moment passed.

When the children were two and a half years old, it became customary to take them to the recreation hall and let them play together under the supervision of a few parents and psychologists. Kelii Morgan, who had once been a teacher and was now a parent, was often with them.

The children responded to him in their restrained fashion. They were patient when the affectionate Kelii laughed or hugged them impulsively, but they enjoyed the folk stories and myths he had learned from his Welsh and Hawaiian forebears. They responded most to tales of a quest for some great piece of knowledge. They heard the humorous stories too, but never laughed.

Josepha came often to see them at play. The children were already used to each other, having visited each other's homes frequently. They liked new places and had never clung to a parent in fear. But their play seemed to her a solemn affair. She had expected rivalries, fussing over toys, laughter, teasing, a few tears.

Instead, she saw red-headed Nenum taking apart a toy space city, peering at the different levels and at the tiny painted lake and trees at its center while Ramli looked on. When Ramli grabbed one level, Josepha expected Nenum to become possessive. But the two began to reassemble it together, whispering all the while.

She saw Teno play with a set of Russian dolls, removing each wooden doll from a larger one until the smallest doll was discovered. When Dawli, the frail-looking child of Teofilo Schmidt, came to Teno's side, Teno willingly yielded the dolls and crawled off in search of another toy.

It was all strange to her. If one played alone, it was because the child wanted to be alone, not because the others left the child out. Josepha searched for tears or the formation of childish cliques, and saw only inquisitiveness and cooperation. Even the muscular, big-boned Kelii, who seemed to be their favorite adult, got no special affection. If he held a picture book on his spacious lap, a child might climb up and sit there, but only to see the illustrations more clearly.

They never misbehaved, at least not in the normal way. If a child wandered off, pursued shortly by a worried parent or psychologist, the young one was usually found investigating a plant or a toy or how a toilet worked. If they were told not to play with the computers until they were shown how to push the buttons, they listened, asked questions, and tried to understand the machines.

On one occasion, Ramli had punched Teno in the stomach. Teno had retaliated with a blow to the arm. Each cried out in pain as Josepha, worried and at the same time almost relieved by the show of normality, rose to her feet to stop it. But the battle was over. The two had learned that violence caused pain.

Although she tried to ignore it, she often felt frustrated. Chane had become more withdrawn, making frequent calls to old friends late at night behind the closed doors of his study. The children could not reward her love with spontaneous displays of affection. She wondered how long it would be before a parent, bewildered by the lack of any real emotional contact with a child, might lash out at one of them.

Josepha and Chane sat in the park with their children. The spring day was unseasonably warm, the blue sky cloudless. A week ago, a third birthday celebration had been held for all the children. The adults had been sociable and gregarious, the young ones solemn and bemused.

Teno and Ramli knelt on the grass, playing an elaborate game with marbles and pebbles; only they knew its rules. Twenty meters away, under an elm, Edwin Joreme lay on a brown blanket with his head on Gurit Stern's lap. Edwin's

The Renewal

child Linsay poked at the grass with a stick. Gurit had apparently left Aleph, her child, at home.

Edwin was a thin man with ash blond hair who looked almost adolescent. Gurit, auburn-haired, green-eyed, and stocky, was one of the few in the village who still intimidated Josepha. Gurit had been a soldier before the Transition. Although she seemed a friendly, hearty sort, there was something hard in her, a toughness, a competence that made Josepha ill at ease. Watching Gurit, she thought of what the woman must have seen and imagined that she was one who probably savored her extended life instead of simply accepting it.

Edwin sat up and moved closer to Linsay. He spoke to the child; Linsay listened, then returned to probing the ground. Josepha thought that Gurit might have passed as the mother of both. Lines creased her face at eyes and mouth, and in the bright afternoon sunlight one clearly saw the gray hairs framing her face. Chane had once asked Gurit why she had not wanted a more youthful appearance. She had laughed, saying she got tired of seeing young faces all the time.

Edwin was still trying to distract Linsay, murmuring to the child intently. Josepha turned to Chane. He had brought some notes with him, but she did not know what they were about. He was ignoring them, gazing absently in the children's direction.

"Is something wrong?" she asked.

He shook his head.

"What are the notes for?" They were written in Italian and Swahili, two languages she did not know.

He was silent for a few moments before replying. "Just some reminiscences, personal things, incidents I might otherwise forget."

"Can't you just consult the computer records?"

"Those are public records, Josepha. They tell nothing of subjective attitudes or personal reactions. And several incidents aren't recorded." His lowered eyelids hid his dark eyes from her.

Impulsively, she touched his arm. Then she heard a cry, a thin, piercing wail.

Edwin was shaking Linsay, muttering under his breath at the child. Linsay wailed. Josepha froze, not understanding what was happening. Chane jumped to his feet, his red caftan swirling around his ankles.

Gurit quickly grabbed Edwin's arms. "Stop it," she said firmly. "What's the matter with you?" He pushed her away violently. Trembling, he stared at his child and then, shockingly, slapped Linsay.

Josepha tensed at the sound. "Why can't you respond?" Edwin was shouting. "I'm sick to death of it, you're as bad as a robot, not the slightest human feeling—"

Gurit again seized Edwin, holding him tightly, and this time he was unable to break away from her strong arms. He crumpled against her. Linsay sat calmly, blond head tilted to one side.

Josepha got up. "I think we should go," she murmured to Chane, feeling that Edwin would not want them to witness any more. Teno and Ramli had stopped playing and were staring at Edwin, fascinated. Josepha thought wearily of all the questions she and Chane would have to answer later.

"We're going home," she said to the children.

3

A small death had entered their lives. Josepha and the children were burying the cat.

They had walked to the woods north of the village and stopped at a weedy clearing. Josepha wore a silvery lifesuit under her gray tunic; she always wore the protective garment when in the forest. She stood under a maple tree, shaded from the summer heat, while Teno and Ramli placed the small furry body in the grave they had dug. The children were dressed only in sleeveless yellow shirts and green shorts. Their stronger bones and muscles did not need lifesuit protection.

The children were seven now. Their rapid growth and the cat's death made Josepha feel she was aging. She could no longer suspend time by living in a permanent eternal stability. Her child had been a toddler so recently. Now Teno was a student, learning to read and calculate or going off with Kelii and a few parents to the lake for a day or two to learn about the outdoors.

Teno was more of a companion to her as well. The child would ask questions about the desk computer, a sandwich, the lilac tree outside, about Ramli and Chane, about what parents were, and after Josepha had explained about Krol, questions about death. The child never smiled, never frowned. Josepha would see only expressions of thoughtfulness, concentration, curiosity, puzzlement.

Ramli and Teno began to cover the cat with dirt and leaves. They had kept the animal for three years; Chane felt that having pets was good for children. They had named the orange and white cat Pericles. Josepha loved animals but had never kept a dog or cat before, knowing that eventually the creature would die. It had been easier, when she lived alone, to watch the robins return to the trees, or the geese fly back to her pond after their migration. She could imagine that the same birds were returning.

The children got along with Pericles in their solemn way. They had learned that tweaking his tail caused him pain and that he would repay any affront to his feline dignity with a baleful stare and the swipe of a paw. They had cleaned out his box, scratched him behind the ears so he would purr, and protected him from the forays of Kaveri Dananda's cocker spaniel Kali, although Josepha had always felt that Kali, despite the ferocity of her name, was frightened of the cat.

But they had also learned that Pericles would kill. Josepha had not always been able to hide the small birds who were victims from the children. It had been hard for her to explain the cruelties of nature and the instincts of animals that even humankind had not fully escaped. The children had listened and absorbed the information, but she did not know if they were reconciled to it.

Now Pericles was dead. He had disappeared for a few days, to be discovered by Chane near the woods outside the village this morning. The small furry body he had carried home had been unmarked. Josepha, seeing it, had wanted to cry. The children did not cry. Heartlessly, it seemed, they had the computer link sensor scan the body to determine the cause of death, which had been, oddly enough, kidney failure. Then Ramli had kindly suggested that they bury the creature in the woods he had loved.

The children had finished. Josepha went to them and they stood by the grave silently for a few minutes, then

The Renewal

began to walk slowly back toward the village.

"Do cats always die?" Teno asked.

"All animals do sooner or later."

"From accidents?"

"Sometimes. Other times it's disease, or getting old." She did not like discussing these matters, but there was no point in shielding the children from them.

"Some people die from accidents too," Teno said emphatically.

"They don't have to," she replied quickly. "If the medical robots get to them in time they don't, and usually they reach them in time because of the Bond, that's why we all wear them."

"Some people want to die," Ramli said loftily. Josepha was too startled to reply. "I saw about it. They kill themselves or sometimes they kill somebody else or ask somebody to do it and they fix their Bonds so they don't find them in time."

"I know that," Teno replied. "I saw a dead guy on the holo, he shot himself and there was blood all over, he put a bullet right in his head and they couldn't bring him back."

Josepha felt sick. She wanted to tell them not to use words like kill, but that would only turn it into a potent obscenity for them. She wished Chane were here instead of home getting dinner ready. "Where did you see such a thing?" she said, trying to keep her voice steady. "You couldn't have seen it at home or at school."

"Over at Nenum's," Teno said.

"Don't lie to me," she answered harshly, stopping along the narrow path and turning to confront them. "Warner and Vladislav wouldn't allow it."

"Nenum knows how to override."

She could read no expression in Teno's gray eyes or

Ramli's black ones. She wanted to get angry, be firm, forbid them to look at such things again, but knew it would do no good. It would only make them more curious.

"Why do they want to die?" Ramli asked.

Josepha shook her head. "It's hard to explain. Sometimes they're unhappy or just tired of everything or . . . people like us used to die, you know that. Many of us still don't know how to handle long lives."

"That's dumb," Ramli said tonelessly. "I want to find out everything and it'll take forever. I don't want to die."

She smiled at them. "Of course you don't." She motioned to them and they resumed walking.

"Is Pericles a ghost?" Teno inquired.

"Where did you hear about ghosts?"

"Kelii told us stories about them. They're dead people except they're ghosts, and you can't see them except sometimes."

She recalled the voice that had spoken to her years ago and was silent. "Are there ghosts, Josepha?" her child said.

"What do you think?"

"I don't think there are any."

"Kelii says it's made-up stuff," Ramli said. "He says people made it up because they didn't know anything. I said if I didn't know I'd find out, I wouldn't make it up."

"Did you ever see a ghost, Josepha?" Teno asked.

"How can she see one if there aren't any," Ramli muttered.

"She can think she did."

"No," she responded, feeling that she was being honest only technically. She could not explain her own experience and conviction until they were older, though she doubted they would understand her even then.

She thought of all the deaths she had seen and suddenly

felt very old, too old to be raising children. The responsibility weighed heavily on her. The decisions were too difficult, the mistakes too frequent. She remembered her own father and mother and the problems they had encountered with her and her brother Charles. Her parents had died in an auto accident a few years after she had married Gene Kolodny. But she had been estranged from them long before, deeply resenting them for reasons never fully understood, knowing she had failed them in some undefined manner but afraid to find out how. After their deaths, filled with guilt and regrets about things left unsaid and undone, she had been forced to put them out of her mind.

They reached the edge of the forest and looked out at the village. The paths were filled with strollers; others sat on the front porches sipping cool drinks. Josepha looked down at Teno and realized that now she could think about her mother and father without the old feelings. It was as if she had a bond with them through the child, as if she was no longer cut off from them even by death.

"It's fair," Teno said suddenly, interrupting her reverie.

"What's fair?"

"Pericles dying. He killed things and now he's dead."

More visitors now came to the village. They had been arriving ever since the children's birth.

There had once been talk of raising the young ones with other, "normal" children, but nothing had come of it. Josepha supposed that it was too late to do anything about it. The visiting children from outside, however curious they might be at first, soon learned that the children here were uninterested in their games, pranks, emotional displays, and rivalries. The visits ended with each group of children keeping to itself.

A few biologists and psychologists came, but most of the visitors were simply curious. Now that the children were older, and the differences between them and the rest of humankind were more obvious, more outsiders arrived. They peered into the recreation hall at Kelii and the children. They went down to the lake where the young ones were being taught to swim. The children bore up well under this inquisitiveness, being even more courteous and well behaved while under observation. Josepha sensed, however, that the visitors might have preferred seeing the children scream or yell or laugh or cry or gang up on someone.

She saw Chane standing with Edwin Joreme and a group of visitors, ten tall Tartars who had congregated in front of Merripen Allen's small cottage. They had just arrived; Chane had accompanied them to the village.

He had been visiting old friends. She had urged him to get away for a few weeks, remembering how refreshed she had felt after a solitary sojourn at her old home. But he looked weary to her. She waved at him and bowed to the Tartars, who bowed back.

Chane seemed surprised to see her. He made his farewells to the visitors and came toward her, greeting her with a light kiss on her forehead. "I didn't expect you to meet me," he said.

"We missed you." She took his arm and they began to walk through the park toward their house. The dark gray sky seemed to hang over them and the brown grass, scattered with red and yellow leaves, was desolate. Chane shivered slightly in his long gray coat. Edwin had taken charge of the visitors, leading them over toward the recreation hall. Josepha recalled the day he had struck Linsay; since then, he had become one of the gentlest and most patient parents here. She could only wonder at what it cost him. His hazel eyes were often doubt-filled and distant.

"Were there many visitors here while I was away?" Chane asked.

"Indeed there were. Didn't I mention it to you when you called? Maybe I didn't."

"I don't think you did."

"Well, don't worry about them, Chane, everyone pretty much ignores them now."

"I have good reason for worrying. I'm even more concerned after being outside. Before, when I called my friends, I was sure they were exaggerating the suspicion and hostility of others toward this community. Now I know they weren't."

She felt a slight prickle of fear. "What are they upset about? What can possibly happen here?"

"They're afraid of the children, of what they might become."

"But that's so silly. What could they do? If anything, the kids should be afraid of us. That is, if they could feel fear. I don't know if they can."

"Granted, it's foolish," Chane replied. "But you've seen the visitors here. They all act a bit apprehensive. The group I came back here with did. I don't understand Russian or Tartar, but I saw that much. And that's nothing compared to what I've seen elsewhere. Those who come here at least give us the benefit of a doubt." He sighed. "People don't want things to change," he murmured, as if speaking to himself.

She was silent. They approached the house and stopped at the gate. "Are Teno and Ramli home?" Chane asked apprehensively.

"They're over at the hall."

They entered the house, hanging their coats in the

hallway. Chane went to the living room and sat on the sofa; he sprawled, head forward, feet out. "I heard one rather interesting proposal," he said as she came into the room and sat next to him. "Some believe that the children should be taken away from here."

"Taken away!" She clasped his hand tightly.

"There was talk of exile, putting them on a colony out by Saturn or some such place."

Josepha was stunned. Recently various groups had started to send murderers and other very disturbed people out to small space colonies under robotic guards. Eventually, it was hoped, they would be aided by new biological or psychological techniques. In reality, they were usually forgotten. Josepha doubted that anything much would ever be done for them. It was small wonder so many murderers attempted suicide rather than risking such an exile.

"But the children aren't criminals," she said. "They've done nothing. Sending them away would only guarantee their bitterness. How are they going to feel about people who would do that to them? They might, in their reasonable way, decide that they have to defend themselves."

"I said that. If they're exiled now, though, so the idea goes, there's not much they can do, they're only children. And once they're gone, there's nothing they can do anyway if they're guarded. I argued with a lot of people, Josepha. I didn't get far." He withdrew his hand and looked away.

She suddenly wanted to hurry to the hall and make sure Teno and Ramli were safe. Instead, she leaned back and closed her eyes. The village had become a fortress, a settlement surrounded by danger, uncertainty, hostility. The visitors were members of reconnaissance missions, spies, enemies.

The Renewal

★ ★ ★ ★ ★

Teno sat on the floor, placing furniture inside a small doll house. Josepha sprawled on Teno's bed, watching the solemn eight-year-old arrange the tiny sofa and chairs Chane had carved. Little figurines lay next to the child—a small mahogany Chane in a red robe, a tiny Josepha with waist-length black hair, and two smaller dolls.

"Two kids from outside were at the hall today," Teno said. "I don't think they liked me." The child's tones were quiet and measured.

"Why do you say that?"

"I could tell when I talked to them."

Josepha peered at Teno. The child's eyes were hidden by long dark lashes. "Did you like them?"

Teno shrugged. "I don't know. Kelii told me I could show them the garden so we went outside, but then the boy said to go around the side of the hall, so I did, and then the girl said for me to take down my pants."

"She said what?" Josepha said, trying not to look too shocked.

"Take down my pants. She said they wanted to see me there and I said I would if they would, so they showed me theirs and I showed them mine and they said I was a freak."

She wanted to reach over and hug the child, but Teno seemed calm and undisturbed. "What happened then, dear?" she managed to ask.

"I said I wasn't and I liked having a penis and vagina and they only had half of what I had and I don't think they liked that. Then the boy said a lot of people didn't like us because we were different from them and I said that was stupid because everybody's a little different from everybody else. I think he was going to hit me but he didn't, and we went back inside."

Josepha sat up on the bed, folding her legs under her. "Do things like that bother you, Teno?"

"No, it's just dumb." The child picked up the Chane doll and put it inside the house.

"Listen," she said quickly, "maybe all of us can go down to the lake this weekend and take out the sailboat. Would you like that?"

"You forgot, we have a camping test then." The children were going to be set loose in the forests beneath the nearby mountains for three days, with only a knife, compass, and poncho each. The young ones were well prepared; they were all skilled campers and robots in the area would be alert to any danger. But Josepha found herself worrying anyway.

"Tell me," she murmured, "why are you so interested in campcraft?"

"We all are."

"I know that." It was one of their peculiarities. Although the children varied in their interests and aptitudes—Teno enjoyed mathematics while Ramli preferred botany—they always remained interested in what all the others were doing. It was as if they thought that if one was interested in something, it might be worthwhile for all of them. "I didn't ask that," Josepha went on. "I asked why *you* were interested."

"It's fun. I like to go and watch the deer, but you have to sneak up on them or they run away. I like to watch the campfire when we sit around. Anyway, we need to know that stuff."

"Why?"

"I might have to live in the woods. Lucky we don't need as much food as you, so we wouldn't have to hunt anything. We could stay a long time."

"Why would you have to live in the woods that way?"

"Maybe they won't let us live anywhere else and we'll have to hide."

"Who won't?"

"The people that don't like us." Teno picked up the Josepha doll and held it.

"Teno," Josepha said quietly, "do you mind it, being different?"

The gray eyes gazed steadily at her. "No. I'm the way I am, I'm me," the child said calmly.

Josepha saw the woman before Alf Heldstrom did.

She and Alf were designing a history course for the children. Even with the computer's aid, the project was more difficult than they had expected. They were arguing over how to present the history of the Transition when Josepha noticed that a woman, an outsider, was watching them.

The visitor was standing under a nearby weeping willow. She was thin, almost emaciated. Her pale platinum hair was clipped short.

"Have you seen that woman before?" Josepha whispered to Alf.

"Never." Alf brushed a wavy lock of long golden hair off his delicate face. "She seems to be alone, usually visitors come in groups."

"It may be silly, but I don't like the way she's looking at us."

The woman walked toward them. Josepha felt apprehensive. She nodded and the blonde woman nodded back. She stood in front of them, nervously pulling at the sleeve of her blue jacket.

"Hello," the woman said softly. "Are you parents?"

Josepha was startled by the directness of the question.

She glanced at Alf. He raised an eyebrow and stared back blankly with his blue eyes. She turned back to the visitor. "Yes," she replied.

Alf uncrossed his legs and sat up. He and the woman stared silently at each other while Josepha tried to keep from fidgeting. At last the woman looked away. "I'm Nola Reann," she said to the air, speaking so softly that Josepha had to lean forward to catch the name. "Where are the children?" She looked at Josepha.

"Camping."

"Camping. I can't imagine why."

"I'm Josepha Ryba. This is Alf Heldstrom. Won't you sit down?"

"Thank you. I'll stand." Nola Reann put her hands inside the pockets of the blue jacket she wore over her silver lifesuit.

"Most of the people who come here are biologists or psychologists," Alf said, in an obvious effort to relieve their discomfort. "We do, of course, get a cross-section of other types too."

"I'm a meteorologist. I'm in space most of the time."

"What did you do before that?"

"I didn't do anything before that. I'm only twenty."

Josepha glanced at Alf, who seemed as surprised as she was. It was easy to forget that there were young people in the world. She tried to recall what it felt like to be twenty.

"Are you here to study the weather?" Alf asked as Josepha attempted to decide if he was being courteous or sarcastic.

"No." Nola swayed on her feet as she surveyed the village. Her dark eyes betrayed her uneasiness. She seemed oddly impatient. She had not lived long enough, Josepha supposed, to be anything else. "What are you trying to do here?" the young woman said suddenly.

"I beg your pardon," Alf murmured.

"What are you trying to do here?"

"We're trying," Josepha answered calmly, "to raise our children."

"Why these children? They're not even normal, they're alien and soulless."

"I *beg* your *pardon*," Alf said harshly. "You have no right to say that. Do you know them? Have you seen them or talked to them?"

"I've seen them on the holo. That's all I need to see. You don't know what you're doing."

"You have no right to say that," Josepha replied. "You have no right to come here and discuss our children in such a hostile way."

Nola Reann stepped back. "Hostile! I'm not hostile. Your biologists are hostile, enemies of the human body and what it represents. They want to change it and mold it, it's only dead matter to them, meat, if you will. They want to change it because they hate it, which means they must hate themselves on some level."

Josepha thought of Merripen. "Tell me," Alf said, smiling slightly, "since you're a meteorologist, how you rationalize the implants I know you have, the ones that provide you with a direct link to the machines you need to do your work."

Nola glared. "That's not the same thing at all. Such devices merely amplify the potential of the human form and mind." She waved her right hand in a gesture of dismissal.

"And your human form could not even be standing here in front of us without the aid of an exoskeleton," Alf went on. Josepha squinted, noticing for the first time the slender silver wires on Nola's hand and the metal support around her neck, partially concealed by her high-collared blue jacket. The woman, she realized, had spent her life either on the moon or in a low-gravity colony. For a moment, she felt sorry for her, but that was as patronizing and wrong as Nola's feelings about the children.

"Do you have any idea," Alf was saying, "what people three hundred years ago might have thought of you?"

Nola smiled, once again hiding her hands in her pockets. "I'm still a human being. I think like you, I feel like you. Everything I use simply aids me in achieving my full potential. I don't lack emotions or sexuality as your children do." She turned her head and looked at Josepha with conviction. "Extended life has at last made it possible for us to become fully human. We can be everything a human being can be. There is no other point to life. These children insult us by saying that we cannot succeed as we are."

"How strange," Josepha said. "If I reasoned the way you do, I might conclude that extended life denied us our humanity by denying us death." She forced out the words with difficulty. "Some people obviously do feel that way."

"You mean murderers and suicides," Nola said blatantly. "I quarrel only with the means they use. They anticipate death, that is all, reach for it prematurely instead of awaiting its eventual arrival. Of course, murder and suicide are at least human talents."

"So is rationality," Alf said.

"What is reason without the fuel of the emotions, the tension between the two that makes all achievement possible? A dead, soulless thing." Nola lowered her voice. "Your biologists are trying to cloak their despair by creating these new beings. They're not giving us a chance to succeed as we are."

"Are you a meteorologist or a missionary?" Alf asked,

raising an eyebrow. "Do you think the human body is sacrosanct? It's only nature's set of compromises. People have been trying to alter it in small ways, either for aesthetic or practical reasons, for centuries."

"Not this drastically." Nola paused, as if at a loss. "It's a mistake."

Josepha thought: there's nothing more to say, we won't even know if we were right or wrong for a long time.

Nola Reann turned and strode away quickly, without a farewell. Josepha moved closer to Alf. "She's unusual, isn't she?" she said softly. "Others aren't like that."

"Do you talk with many people elsewhere?"

She shook her head.

"She may be extreme, but she's not all that unusual."

"What will they do?"

He sighed. "I don't know. There's not really much they can do."

Josepha looked up and gazed past the park. Behind the houses ahead, robot guards patrolled the grounds. There were more guards lately.

Teno and Ramli were playing with four other children in the living room. Josepha could hear them from her study: Teno's inflections, Ramli's slight drawl, Nenum's murmur, Aleph's rasp, Yoshi's sing-song, Linsay's guttural throat noises. They had already passed their wilderness survival test, although it would hardly have mattered if they had not. Unobtrusive robots had been near them at all times. The village had held a celebration for the children when they returned, but the ceremony had meant more to the parents than to the young ones, who seemed content with success alone.

She did not mind the noise, although there was more of

it than usual. She paid it little attention as she sat at her desk, watching the final history syllabus roll by on her reader screen. If neither she nor Alf had anything further to add, they would finalize it, show it to a teacher, then program the computer.

She tried to concentrate, not wanting to think of Chane. He and Warner Chavez had gone to one of the lodges for the day. She felt a pang at the thought. Vladislav, still living with Warner, had taken up with Chen Li Hua some time ago. Warner began seeing Chane a while later.

Chane had not tried to deceive her and she had made no objections. Yet even after two months of this, Josepha still felt twinges. At least Warner and Vladislav knew how they felt about each other. Josepha knew only that she would be hurt if she lost Chane and that she missed him when he was not with her. But she did not know what he felt. Oddly enough, their lovemaking had improved. Jealousy was always a good aphrodisiac, but the price was too high.

She sighed. She and Chane had lived in isolation from each other since the very beginning. Except for the children and their upbringing, they shared very little of real substance. Their other obligations and pursuits bad been carefully divided into equal portions, everything from rooms to housework to time alone to time with friends. There had been nothing strange about that; it seemed reasonable and practical.

But, looking back, she felt as if she had deceived herself. People grew closer, or changed, or grew apart; they were not capable of maintaining the same static arrangements day after day, year after year. Josepha, afraid to admit it to herself before, now knew that she was coming to love Chane.

She put her hands, palms down, on the reader's flat surface. She did not want to be alone anymore, surrounded by walls of sensible arrangements which protected only a solitary mind reflecting endlessly on itself and its own uniqueness. She had deluded herself by thinking that she could preserve those barriers in this village. The children had already penetrated them, binding her to the future and the past.

She recalled her pre-Transition life. It had not been that unusual in its isolation from family, demanding relationships, and any sense of continuity. The techniques guaranteeing personal immortality had preserved the individualistic society in which she had lived. Without that development, her fragmenting culture might well have been overrun by those who were unified and bound together in a common purpose. Only the attainment of the ancient dream of eternal life had been enough to save her culture and conquer the others as well. Small wonder, she thought, that Nola Reann and those like her felt threatened by the children, whose existence once more questioned everything.

The sound of a laugh startled her. She sat up and pushed the reader to one side. The laugh was hollow, devoid of merriment. She got up and walked softly out of the study, peering around the stairway into the living room.

The children were talking, lounging in various uncharacteristic attitudes around the room. Nenum stood slouching, hands on hips, looking quite pretty. A peculiar whine had crept into the child's voice that seemed familiar.

"I don't *know* why," Nenum was saying, tucking a short lock of reddish hair behind an ear. "I just feel depressed, you know, everything seems . . ." Josepha recognized the voice of Warner and the words of one of her common complaints.

Teno ambled over to Nenum. Her child's face was contorted in an odd expression, eyes wide, mouth pulled down. "Don't worry," Teno said, putting a hand on Nenum's shoulder. "Ah, you need a mood and you'll feel better. Uh, sometimes I feel that way myself. It'll go away."

"Why don't we have a party?" Aleph said, mimicking Gurit's tones. "I haven't tied one on in a while."

"I have a headache," Linsay growled, stomping fiercely around the room. Josepha recognized the tense but controlled voice of Edwin Joreme. "They get to me sometimes, they get to me."

"Oh, Edwin," Teno replied, "you don't mean that, ah, I know you. You *dote* on Linsay." Josepha heard herself, the pauses, the hesitation, the rising inflection at the end of sentences, and shrank back near the wall. Was that how she sounded, that silly mixture of meliorism and insecurity? Was that how they all sounded? She wanted to tiptoe back to the study, but puzzlement and curiosity held her as she listened:

RAMLI (*firmly*): Don't worry, I just have to make two calls, I won't be on long. Then we'll go. Why get there early?

TENO: I know I shouldn't, but, uh, I always feel so silly there. Li Hua's so intelligent she always makes me feel ignorant.

ALEPH: You know what I think? We could do with some tough times again. Builds character. Everyone's getting soft. If we had some hardships, a lot of people wouldn't make it.

NENUM (*whining*): I get depressed when I hear that. You're a hard person.

YOSHI (*gruffly*): The last time I was on Asgard, I noticed an interesting refinement in their holo transmissions.

The Renewal

LINSAY: Not *again*. Do we have to listen to that *again?*
TENO: Now don't be so rude.

Josepha peered around the staircase once more, still hidden in the shadows. She felt like a spy. Ramli was sitting on the sofa slouched over, feet extended. Teno fluttered around the room nervously, looking very pretty and very insecure. Nenum lounged in the corner, gazing seductively at Ramli. Pained by the too-familiar scene, Josepha closed her eyes for a moment.

When she opened them, the children were themselves, seated on the floor, arms folded, murmuring softly. "I don't understand it," Teno said clearly.

"It's the way they are," Aleph replied. "You know that. They're confused."

"That's not what I meant. They wanted us to be different from them, right?" Teno paused. "That means they wanted us to be better. So if they think we're better, then why don't they act more like us?"

"You know why," Linsay said. "They can't help it. Their bodies are different. They like feelings, but they lie about them too. They lie about sex the most."

"Well, I don't know why people like to think things that aren't true. When I touch myself or Ramli does, it feels nice and that's all, but they act as if it's the most important thing in the world."

"It must feel different to them," Nenum muttered.

"But they made us so we're different," Teno said. "I don't think they like themselves the way they are. And if they liked us, they'd try to be like us. They have minds, they can think. So if they aren't like us, it has to be because they can't help it and their feelings are stronger, or it's because they don't like the way we are either."

"But they made us this way," Ramli responded.

"We're an experiment. Experiments don't always work."

Josepha crept back to her study, knowing she had eavesdropped too long. She paused at her desk, remembering the calmness in the young voices as well as the eerie precision with which they had imitated the adults. The voices had lacked both humor and contempt. They had only been trying to make sense of their parents' behavior.

She wondered what else the children might be concluding about them.

Josepha shivered slightly in her light jumpsuit and jacket. Gurit Stern stood with her. The weather was cooler; before them, the lake rippled. The water was calmer near the shore; farther out, the wind was whipping up whitecaps.

Aleph, Teno, and Ramli were on the dock, tying up the canoe they had taken out that morning. The young ones had wisely decided not to stay out on the lake. There was still time to have a meal inside one of the lodges before going back to the village.

Gurit, dressed only in a beige short-sleeved shirt and brown slacks, did not seem to feel cold. She smiled sympathetically at Josepha, then walked out onto the dock to make certain the canoe had been tied up properly. There was really no need to check. The children usually made only one mistake before learning a skill.

She was wondering idly whether they should turn the canoe over on the dock instead when she heard a voice. "Josepha!" She turned and saw Warner and Nenum scurrying down the hill toward the lake. She waved at them.

"I didn't think anyone would be out here today," Warner called as she came nearer.

Josepha smiled. "No one else is. Believe me, we

wouldn't be either if we'd known it was going to be this cold."

Warner, dressed warmly in a red coat, smiled back. Nenum hurried down to the dock to greet the others. "We thought that as long as we've walked this far, we might as well eat before going home."

"We were just about to have lunch ourselves." Warner's eyes did not meet hers. "You must join us," Josepha continued. "I miss you, I don't see you as much lately."

"I wasn't sure if you wanted to."

"Oh, Warner. You're my friend." Josepha took Warner's arm as they began to climb the stone steps which led to the lodge, a large log cabin surrounded by evergreens.

"He loves you, Jo." Josepha, startled, let go of her friend. "What do you mean?"

"I can tell. He hasn't said so, but it's obvious. I think he's afraid to tell you, I don't know why. Maybe he's not sure how you'll take it."

She was about to reply when she saw something move in the woods ahead. A man stepped from behind the trees. He was looking down toward the lake. He was dressed entirely in white; there were dirt and grass stains on his knees. He held his hands behind him, as if concealing something. Thick, dark, shoulder-length hair hung around his face.

He stood fifteen meters above them without moving. Josepha stopped and glanced quickly at Warner.

"Visitor?" Warner murmured.

"Alone? Out here?" Josepha looked back at the man. Farther up the hill behind him, a small robot moved swiftly toward the stranger on its treads. And then the man quickly raised his arm and she saw the weapon, a small silver cylinder.

He aimed. She heard Gurit scream: "Get down!" A beam of light flashed from the weapon.

Josepha turned numbly. Gurit had thrown herself over one child's body, two others lay near her, the fourth . . . something was wrong with the fourth. There was another flash of light, shocking her out of the paralysis that had settled over her. She looked back.

The man's headless torso toppled over into the foliage. For a moment she thought the robot had fired on him; then she realized the man had turned his weapon on himself. The robot reached his side and stood there helplessly, too late.

She turned to Warner. Her friend's head shook from side to side soundlessly. She held out her hands to Josepha, then spun around and began to run down to the children. Josepha followed her.

Gurit stood up, her hands on Ramli's shoulders. Teno, still lying on the ground, looked up. Josepha thought: they're safe, they're all right.

Gurit reached out to Aleph and pulled her child near her. But another small body did not move. Josepha suddenly realized that she could not see Nenum's red hair. Warner was running to the small body.

Josepha rushed to her friend, throwing her arms around Warner. "Don't," she managed to say. Warner pulled away and finally stood over her child.

Nenum too was beyond revival, head burned off by the visitor's weapon. Nenum's mother was silent, clenching and unclenching her fists, shaking her head, staring at Josepha with black, frightened eyes. Josepha opened her mouth and found she had no voice. Her knees buckled and she sat down hard on the ground, hugging her legs with her arms. Dimly, she saw Gurit go to Warner.

Warner began to wail. Gurit held her. Aleph observed them with pale green eyes. Josepha drew her legs closer to her chest.

Teno and Ramli were standing over her. She thought: we should go, I can't keep them here with this, what do I say, how can I explain it? Fear swept over her and she found herself shaking. Teno reached out and held her hands until she stopped.

Others, she knew, would be there soon. The robot had probably already signaled to them. The machine intelligence, having failed to protect them, waited on the hill, its head slowly spinning as it continued to survey the woods. It held the weapon in its metal fist. The children were silent, watching her with calm, questioning eyes.

Josepha wound her way past the cots and mats, trying not to disturb the children who lay on them. The young ones had been living here in the recreation hall for a week, always watched, never left alone nor allowed to wander. Two robots stood in the back of the room; another was posted near a doorway.

Kelii Morgan sat in a straight-backed chair near the mat where his child Alani was sleeping. He was unarmed; the robots would stun anyone entering the room with a weapon. She motioned to him. He did not move. The children slept, breathing rhythmically. They had not rebelled against the restrictions placed on them.

She moved closer to Kelii. "Should we go downstairs now?" she whispered. Alani stirred slightly. Kelii leaned over and adjusted the child's blanket.

"I'll stay here," he replied softly. "Go on, Josepha, you can tell me what happened later on."

"Sure you don't want company?"

"Go on, it's all right. I want to be here in case one of them wakes up."

She left the room and hurried down the ramp. Below, in

the room where the children usually played and studied, parents sat among the desks, computer consoles, tables, and chairs. Most of them sat on the floor. A few were on benches near the walls. Here three robots also stood guard, and she knew that there were others outside.

Chen Li Hua, who had taken it upon herself to call the parents together, stood under the screen in the front of the room. "Where's Kelii?" she asked in her flat, hoarse voice.

"He wants to stay upstairs."

"Then we might as well start, and I'll say what I have to say."

Josepha saw Chane near the doorway and made her way to him, sitting down next to him on the floor. "Where's Merripen?" a man asked, and she recognized the voice of Edwin Joreme.

"I didn't ask him," Li Hua replied. "I didn't ask anyone except parents to come here tonight. If any of the others arrive, as I suppose they might, that's fine, but I think any decisions we make should be ours." She cleared her throat and squinted; her eyes became slits. "Some of us have been asking for better security here all along, for restrictions on visitors, for supervision of any stranger who came here. We allowed ourselves to be talked out of it, supposedly for the good of the children. You see where that got us. It's time we insisted on whatever we think is right." The small woman brushed a hand over her short cap of straight dark hair.

Chane, looking sad and pensive, reached for Josepha's hand and held it. "They're gone," he murmured to her. "I went over to their home and Li Hua told me. They left this morning, before anyone was up."

"Where did they go?"

"I don't know. Vladislav went with two psychologists.

Warner left with a friend who came for her."

She was silent, thinking of what she could have done, what she could have said to Warner and Vladislav, what she had been unable to do. It had not been enough, holding Vladislav while he sobbed, calming Warner, trying to figure out how to bury poor Nenum after skin scrapings had been stored for possible cloning.

Josepha had aided Warner, a stunned almost catatonic Warner, in arranging a small ceremony in the foothills beyond the nearby woods. She, Chane, and Gurit had accompanied Warner and Vladislav. As they stood, watching two robots place the small body in the ground, Josepha realized that the ceremony had been a terrible mistake. They were marking an irrational act, an insane act, completely outside the fabric of their society. They could gain nothing from Nenum's death. The death of any child would have been horrifying enough in former times; even during ages when such deaths were commonplace and expected, there had at least been the hope of a life beyond or the harsher view that the deaths of the weak might make future generations stronger. Their discovery that the murderer had been a man with two suicide attempts to his credit and a confused belief in some of the tenets espoused by people like Nola Reann only made the whole thing more absurd.

Josepha, standing with her friends, had found herself praying, clinging to the hope that the visions she had glimpsed so long ago were real. She wanted to speak of them to Warner and Vladislav, offer them something that would ease their pain. But she kept silent, thinking they would not understand or, worse yet, think she was mocking them with false hopes.

Warner had rejected the idea of raising Nenum's clone and had talked Vladislav out of it too. Instead, she had gone to Merripen, asking him to have the experience removed from her memory. He had called in a psychologist; at last they had agreed. It was a delicate business, this erasing of one's memory, and Josepha knew it would help Warner only in the short run. Her friend would lose the past nine years, but eventually she would become aware of discontinuities, of blank spots, and would attempt to fill them in; the memories, little by little, might return and have to be faced. And in the meantime, a black emptiness would exist in the back of her mind to bother her without her ever being quite sure of what it was until the recollections returned, perhaps wrenchingly, in dreams and disassociated fragments. Better to let time handle it, better to absorb it, face it, and let it fade. Merripen, she was sure, had agreed to the procedure only to assuage his own guilt and sense of failure in his responsibilities. The psychologist should have treated him.

But no psychologist would treat a biologist without the biologist's request. The biologists had created the society and sustained it with their techniques; to question the motivations of one would be to question the society. Eventually, of course, the children, these children of Merripen's mind, might question it and seek to change it, and then Merripen would be held to account, but not yet.

Li Hua was still speaking, apparently answering another question. She paused, and Josepha saw Gurit rise to her feet.

"Listen," the former soldier said firmly, "you have something to tell us and you've been beating around the bush. Make your point, Li Hua."

"Very well. You all know about those who want to exile the children. Now some think we should have raised them with other children from the beginning, but most of us thought that would be a hardship, that there might be animosity or a lack of understanding between the two groups. In any event, we thought it wiser to wait until the children were older, and we did encourage visitors, which was probably a mistake as I see it. The children are better off developing in their own way."

Gurit coughed. "The point, Li Hua, the point."

"I propose that we agree with the proponents of exile, and move to a space colony of our own as soon as possible."

Gurit sat down. Everyone absorbed the statement. A few shook their heads. Amarisa Drew, a tall Eurasian who was one of Yoshi's parents, waved an arm. "How is that going to solve anything?" she asked in her musical voice.

"It will ease the fears of those who distrust the children," Li Hua replied. "Security precautions will be simpler. The children won't have to face hostility. Any latent talents they have can develop more openly. Later, when they're older, they can return or lead out their lives wherever they choose."

"One moment, please," Dawud al-Ahmad called out. "Why should such a measure help? Why wouldn't those who fear the children grow more afraid in their absence? Ignorance is usually a greater spur to fear than knowledge." He tugged at his short beard. "Wisdom cannot grow in isolation."

"There's a practical problem," Kaveri Dananda said, "that you haven't mentioned either."

"And what is that?" Li Hua asked.

Kaveri stood, adjusting her green sari. "What is to prevent a group of the insane from attacking our little colony in space?"

The Chinese woman shook her head. "Such an action requires planning and teamwork, something I hardly think fanatics would be able to do successfully."

"Nonsense," Kaveri replied.

"An isolated attack like the one Josepha and Gurit witnessed is one thing, a concerted attack quite another. Most people now have lost a good deal of the ability to work with others smoothly—we have been cultivating our individuality for too long. Disturbed people have this tendency to an even greater degree."

"But we would be vulnerable," Kaveri said. "And I think you underestimate the driving force of a mad idea deeply held."

"We would have ample warning, we could defend ourselves, and could station ourselves at such a distance from others that we would constitute no threat."

"But we could still be attacked," Dawud said. "Here, at worst, a few of us could survive. In space, we might all . . ." He held out his hands.

Josepha found herself rising to her feet. Nervously, she surveyed the room. Li Hua turned toward her.

"Josepha?"

She cleared her throat. "We're down here talking," Josepha began, "while the children are upstairs under guard. I don't know whether any of them actually feel fear or not, but they'll certainly acquire a good imitation of it if we go on this way. They'll learn to distrust and fear almost everyone if they haven't already. And if they turn into alienated adults as some fear they will, we'll have ourselves to blame, not the madman who shot poor Nenum. This exile will only make it worse for them. The only way we can help them is by returning to some semblance of normal life, here, in our homes, as soon as possible."

"A pretty set of sentiments," Li Hua muttered. "But how do we keep the same thing from happening again?"

"Don't you see?" Josepha focused first on Kaveri, then turned toward Amarisa Drew, hoping for support. "Don't you realize how many people will feel sympathy for us now? Distrust is one thing, murder quite another. If we communicate openly with others, we can win their trust."

"We tried that," Edwin Joreme said from across the room, "and you see what happened. My advice is to have the biologists tell everyone to leave us alone and let them know what might happen if they don't. They're the ones with power."

"You're wrong," Josepha answered. "They don't believe they have much power. Ask Merripen if you don't believe me. And even if they did, that would be no solution, it would create only more hostility." She glanced around. Amarisa, Kaveri, and Dawud were nodding their heads in agreement.

"Li Hua has suggested a specific course of action," Edwin went on. "You have offered only vague possibilities. Give us a course of action. What exactly would you have us do?"

It was a fair question. She did not know how to reply.

Then Chane spoke. "It's obvious," he said in his deep voice. "First, we must invite people to live here if they wish. I'm talking about welcoming them, not the sort of half-hearted tolerance of outsiders we have now. Second, some of us must leave the village for short periods to communicate with others, propagandize them, if you will. I have spoken to many people over the holo, but such a measure does not have the impact of personal, face-to-face communication."

"And who will go?" Lulee Bernard called out, looking like a small, auburn-haired, serious child herself. "Isn't it more important that we stay with our children?"

"Perhaps it is," Chane replied, "although I don't know how much good that'll do them if they have no place in our world."

Several parents nodded their heads, murmuring. "It might be dangerous for the ones who leave," Edwin objected. "Have you thought of that? You can't be protected as well, if at all."

"It's a risk we'll have to take," Chane responded. Josepha saw fear in his eyes. "We have little time to spare for once," he continued. "If we hadn't all grown so slow to act, we would have seen the wisdom of this course a long time ago. Since I brought this up, I'll volunteer my own services, if it's all right with the rest of you."

Josepha felt her muscles tighten. She could not look at Chane. He should have spoken with her before making such an offer. She could not object here in front of everyone and she could not stop him if he wanted to leave.

She thought: Warner was wrong, she was mistaken about Chane loving me, and now I can't even ask her about it. Numbly she listened to the discussion go on, not really hearing any of it.

Josepha gave in; she had no choice. Chane had persuaded the villagers. He would be accompanied by Amarisa Drew and Timmi Akakse, a handsome Jamaican with the habit of changing her name every thirty years or so.

She wanted to argue with Chane, but she did not. Instead she tried to act calmly, explaining to the children why he was leaving them for a bit. They did not seem disturbed, asking only why they could not go as well. She had replied lamely that their studies were more important. But later she heard Teno tell Ramli that the parents were afraid they might be harmed by someone.

Whenever Chane glanced at her, she smiled, perhaps too brightly and reassuringly. The night before he left, he held her in bed and looked directly into her eyes and she knew she had not fooled him at all. She waited for him to ask her how she really felt, hoping she could stem the flow of angry and resentful words that would pour from her, but he did not speak, possibly afraid of what she might say.

She waited until he was ready to leave the next morning, off to join Timmi and Amarisa for a final session with Merripen before departure. Hating herself for speaking at such an awkward time, she heard her words: "You're leaving because of me."

Chane pulled back as if he had been struck. "No," he said finally, placing his hands on her shoulders. She wanted to twist away.

"Yes. First it was Warner and now this. You want to get away."

"You're wrong, Josepha, it has nothing to do with you. There's more to it than you think."

"It might be dangerous," she said, wishing she could stop the pointless argument. He took his hands away and she waited for him to walk out the door.

"I won't be gone that long. I wanted to bring you and the children along, but I know how hard it is for you to meet a lot of strangers. Anyway, you know we decided it just wasn't fair to ask young children, however rational, to defend their existence before people they don't even know."

She was beaten. She forced herself to smile again, to exercise the patience she should have learned during her long life. "I guess I'm being unfair," she murmured. "I'll miss you, but . . ."

"I'll be back before you know it."

He was gone.

She went to the window and watched him stride across the courtyard, closing the gate behind him.

4

Teno was as tall as Josepha, Ramli somewhat taller. They had grown rapidly during the past years. They had retained their sexual ambiguity; slender bodies, slightly broad shoulders, a range of gestures that flowed from the delicate to the clumsy to the athletic. They were strangers.

They had not always been strangers. After Chane had left, Josepha had grown closer to them. She had taught them how to make pottery and how to sketch. She had been delighted when she found that they in turn were teaching these skills to the other children, though she was a bit disappointed with what they produced; accurate, photographically realistic drawings and simple utilitarian plates and vases. She had found at first that as she spent more time with Teno and Ramli, she missed Chane less.

Chane's first trip should have lasted two months. It had stretched into almost half a year. Had he been returning to her alone, it would not have mattered. But the children grew, the life of the village went on. She had consulted him during his calls and the children bantered pleasantly with his image, but Josepha had made the day-to-day decisions. Chane had returned to people who got along perfectly well without him.

He, Amarisa, and Timmi stayed away from the village for longer and longer periods of time. Estranged from their families while apparently having some success on the outside, Josepha knew they found their absences easier to rationalize as time passed. Perhaps they were also telling themselves that there would be time enough to renew their relationships with their children and their lovers after they had succeeded in their outside tasks.

Josepha sat in her favorite chair knitting while Teno and Ramli sprawled on the living room rug, poring over printouts and diagrams. She thought of Chane. She missed him more now, alone in this house with two increasingly impenetrable strangers. The hours she kept filled with new projects, friends, even a new intellectual challenge—she had decided to learn something about microbiology, equipping herself with a microscope and slides—only seemed to make her loneliness worse when she was alone with her thoughts.

She knitted and ruminated, remembering two encounters, realizing again how poorly she had handled both.

One had been with Chane during his first visit home. They had gone sailing on the lake with the children, then enjoyed a quiet dinner by themselves. She had filled him in on the events during his absence. He had told her about some of the understanding people with whom he had spoken.

"Have you become involved with anyone else yet?" he asked her as they sipped their after-dinner brandy.

"Why should I?"

"I don't expect you to deprive yourself simply because I'm away."

"Oh, Chane." She chuckled softly. "I'm used to being by myself, I used to like living that way, you know. You needn't worry about me. I don't need to be involved with another man."

She looked down at the pale green yarn, remembering that comment. She had fancied that she was reassuring Chane. But she had made the remark because of a dimly felt resentment, sure he had not missed the children or her that much; knowing also, since he had not tried to hide it, that he had enjoyed a few casual sexual adventures while away. She had spoken and told herself self-righteously that she would ease him. She had succeeded only in telling him bluntly that she could live alone and be happy about it while at the same time making him feel guilty about his own perfectly natural sexual involvements. She had hurt him, as she had unconsciously intended.

The second encounter had been with Merripen Allen. The biologist had taken to visiting her and the children while Chane was away. She had been sympathetic, knowing that Merripen had grown depressed about the project, feeling that it had escaped his control and that he no longer had anything to say about future events. He was an obsolete functionary wandering about the village, not needed by the children, unnecessary to the parents who had taken matters into their own hands. She knew the visits cheered him up and had been glad of it. But then she had hurt Merripen too.

He had come to her one night. The children were sleeping and she was alone. She offered him some wine but he refused it. Instead, he took her arm and led her to the sofa.

"Let me stay with you tonight, Josepha."

She drew back, surprised. "I can't, Merripen."

"Why not?"

"Well . . . there is . . ."

"Don't be silly. Chane's not denying himself, why should you?"

"I can't explain. It's different for me."

She had been foolish. Her needles clicked; the children chattered. It would have taken so little effort to give Merripen the human contact he had probably needed as much as the sex. And it would have been no sacrifice either;

The Renewal

she had felt a sudden desire for the handsome biologist even as she refused him. Why did I do it? she asked herself silently, but she knew the answer. She did not want emotional risks. Merripen might have wanted a commitment of some kind; for sex alone he could easily have turned elsewhere.

She did not want things this way. She no longer wanted her self-imposed exile from life. She could not do anything about Merripen; she had turned him away for the last time. She wondered if it was too late to do anything about Chane.

Merripen, at least, had now found his way back into village life. All of the children sought him out. He was the only adult they did seek out. The rest of them, even Kelii, were ignored or tolerated.

It had started when the children were eleven. They were not overtly hostile or rebellious, simply more indifferent. Lulee Bernard spoke of not knowing where her child was much of the time; Edwin Joreme, even grumpier than usual, muttered about being told he didn't know much; Gurit Stern complained about being asked embarrassing questions and having her answers rejected out of hand.

The children were thirteen now. She watched them as they sat on the rug surveying diagrams and charts. They were adolescents. She should have expected it. They kept to themselves, cultivating a flat, inexpressive manner of speech, wearing short, clipped hair and simple clothing. All of these new young people were austere in appearance, as if criticizing the more flamboyant and varied garb of their parents.

"What are you looking at so intently?" she asked the children. Neither replied. "What is it?" she said again.

Finally Teno looked up. The child's short hair was curled at the ends, making the face seem almost pretty.

"Ectogenesis chamber," the young one remarked.

"More biology? Is that all you think about?" They were silent. Josepha imagined that Merripen must be gratified by this recent obsession. "Whatever for?"

"See how it works."

"We have to use it someday," Ramli added.

"I know, but you don't seem to pay any attention to anything else," she responded, trying to sound lighthearted. "You spend so little time on your art now, or history, and you used to enjoy those things."

"This is more important," Ramli said tersely.

"I didn't say it wasn't, I just said there are other things."

They remained silent.

"You could at least reply."

"Aren't you supposed to see Gurit this afternoon?" Teno said blandly before turning back to the diagrams.

Josepha felt unaccountably depressed. Of course they were obsessed with biology; for all she knew, it was their substitute for the pair-bonding of normal adolescents. She did not know why they had not paired off; it might have little to do with their physiology. Having been raised together almost as siblings or relatives, the young people were following the pattern normal to such groups by not forming couples. Whether they would form such bonds outside the group remained to be seen.

There were, at any rate, good reasons for this interest in biological techniques. The young ones would not run the risk of natural childbirth even though, theoretically, they were capable of it. If they were to control their own reproduction, they would have to learn what the biologists knew. Perhaps they were also protecting themselves in case at some future time the biologists decided that this "experiment" was a failure.

She watched them, wondering what they might do if they began to think of themselves as an evolutionary dead end. In their rational way, they might simply design another kind of being, one better suited to life than either themselves or the human beings who had raised them.

Josepha thought: we're the dead end. Merripen believed that and he was the person they saw most often now. *We're the dead end.*

Josepha, standing near the gate, noticed the young visitors. There were four, two boys and two girls. They were dressed in shiny, copper-colored suits with high collars. One boy slouched; the other stood straight, hands on hips. One of the girls, tall and muscular, was speaking; she gestured with her arms, flinging them out from the shoulders. The other girl stood on one leg, flexing the other, pointing one foot toward the ground. Teno and Aleph stood listening; they were still as statues. Teno was in a worn brown corduroy jacket and pants and Aleph wore gray overalls.

"What are you staring at?" Chen Li Hua said in her hoarse voice. She sat with her back to the stone wall.

"Nothing. Some visitors, that's all." Josepha swung the gate gently. The hinges no longer squeaked, but the latch was still not working properly.

"As I was saying, Timmi was kind of discouraged about her trip to Madrid. There's a character there who's opposed to almost all biological modifications. Timmi couldn't understand his arguments, she suspects he may have doubts about extended life as well, but he has a following. Well, it just proves that if you use shit for fertilizer something always grows."

Josepha peered at the latch. "Why don't you have a robot fix it?" Li Hua asked.

"I guess I'll have to, this place needs work. One of the solar panels on the roof needs checking and one of my faucets keeps dripping."

"Your homeostat must need fixing too. This house always seemed poorly designed to me."

"Maybe, but I never liked the newer designs, they always seemed—" A movement caught her eye. She looked up and saw the tall, muscular girl pull back her arm. Suddenly she struck Teno. Teno staggered back.

Aleph leapt at the girl. The other copper-clothed outsiders moved in and Josepha could no longer see Aleph's stocky form. "They're fighting," she said uncertainly.

Li Hua got up and came to the gate. Josepha said, "We'd better stop it."

"Don't bother, I think they can take care of themselves. Look." Ramli and three others were running toward the battle. They reached the outsiders and pushed them away, dodging their punches. Teno and Aleph got to their feet. The tall girl and one of the boys moved back in, flailing wildly with their fists. Josepha saw that the village children were fighting defensively, blocking the blows, then pushing the others away.

The outcome, she realized, was not in doubt. There were six villagers to four visitors. Teno and the others also had quicker reflexes and sturdier muscles. They chopped and kicked efficiently. The visitors quickly retreated a few meters and stood together grumbling, nursing their injuries.

The violence sickened Josepha. She pushed the gate open and walked across the park with Li Hua close behind. She passed the outsiders, who seemed curiously unmarked by the fight in spite of their groaning. She reached Teno. One of her child's eyes was discolored. Aleph, Ramli, and the others were scratched and beaten; their clothes were

The Renewal

torn. Yet they had won, or so it seemed.

"What was that all about?" she asked harshly. Teno stared back calmly.

"We had to defend ourselves." The child's voice sounded regretful. "They wouldn't have stopped trying to hurt us unless we did." Josepha spotted the scratches on Aleph's face and an ugly bruise on Ramli's arm. The visitors had tried their best to hurt them, yet the village children had responded only with defensive gestures.

"But how did it start?" she said.

"They don't like us and they're afraid."

Li Hua sighed. "What now?"

"We'd better talk to them," Ramli murmured. "We shouldn't just leave them there."

"It was hardly a fair fight anyway," Li Hua said. "Six against four, and you being stronger."

The young people seemed mystified. "What's fair about a fight?" Aleph asked. "The point is to stop it."

"Let's go," Teno said. They moved past Li Hua and Josepha toward the outsiders.

But the visitors were already leaving the park. Teno called to them; they did not answer. Josepha watched them get into a blue hovercraft parked near Warner's empty house and drive away.

The children had gone camping in the foothills.

Josepha had seen Teno and Ramli off, helping them pack their gear, seeing them meet their friends outside the courtyard. As she watched them stride away in groups of two or three, hands clasped, packs on their slender backs, she had felt tired and old.

There had been no reason to worry. The young people wore Bonds and needed little food and water. But now a week and a half had passed and the children had not returned, nor had they transmitted a message. Josepha, somewhat uneasy, consulted her computer, which indicated that they were still in the foothills.

She called Alf Heldstrom. His image, seated behind a compositor, appeared. "Josepha! Haven't seen you since Lulee's party. Why don't you come over for lunch?"

"I'm worried about the children, Teno and Ramli haven't called in at all. Have you heard anything?"

"You shouldn't worry. They're in the foothills, I know the region, they can take care of themselves."

"I know where they are, I just found out."

"Look, if anything was wrong, an emergency signal would have come in by now."

"Does Merripen know what they're doing?"

Alf shook his head.

She noticed a light flashing on the console. "Alf, someone else is calling, can I get back to you?"

"Sure. Come on over if you like." Alf disappeared and was replaced by the image of Chane.

They exchanged their ritualized greetings. Josepha wanted to reach out to him, mend the rift, but she did not know how to do it. He asked about Ramli and Teno.

"They're not here now. The children all decided to go camping more than a week ago."

"I guess they're all right then."

"I'm sure they are, they haven't called in, but . . . well, I have to admit I'm a little worried."

"Did they say why they were going?"

"No, but . . ."

"Didn't anyone ask?"

"It's hard to ask them anything now, they seem to resent it, if they can resent anything. You'd know that if you . . ."

Josepha caught herself in time. "They're older now, they aren't docile little children."

"So everyone just let them go off."

"Oh, Chane, it isn't as if they aren't prepared or hadn't gone before. If something was wrong, we would have had a signal."

He looked exasperated. "As if nothing could go wrong with their Bonds or they couldn't make a mistake or someone couldn't harm them."

"Who the hell are you to be so concerned?" she burst out at last. "You aren't even here most of the time." She stopped. This was no time to pick a fight with him. "Very well," she continued, "we'll go look for them. I imagine they'll be annoyed with us, or at least puzzled." They might have made an error, she thought. It was too easy to assume that because the young people were rational, they were infallible. "Chane, do you have any appointments today?"

"Late this afternoon."

"Break them. Please come home."

"What for?"

"I thought you were concerned about the kids." She paused. "That isn't the only reason. I miss you."

"I was just there."

"Almost five months ago."

"That's not so long."

"It is, it seems longer here. I miss you."

"You get along pretty well by yourself."

"Yes, I get along by myself, but I don't like it. I get along because, like you and everyone else, I think there'll be plenty of time to take care of things later on. It's a bad habit all of us have. And you see what happens. Later never gets here. I love you, Chane." Her face perspired. Her hands shook. She drew them under her desk where Chane could not see them. "Please come home." She waited, expecting him to smooth it all over while refusing.

"I'll be home tomorrow."

Startled, she gazed at his image silently, then held out a hand to it. "I'll go look for the children," she managed to say. "I'll let you know what's happened."

Josepha, accompanied by Alf and Gurit, glided swiftly over the treetops, surveying the ground below. The belt around her waist was constricting, the jet on her back heavy. But this way they had maneuverability; a vehicle would have restricted their movements. She steered herself carefully as they passed over a small clearing and saw the remains of a campfire, a blackened area surrounded by stones and covered with dirt.

Josepha was frightened now, trying desperately not to give in to panic, not wanting to suspect the worst. Immediately after the call from Chane, she had contacted a robot in the foothills and sent it to where the children should have been. Looking through the robot's eyes, her screen had shown only a deserted clearing while the computer told her that the young people were not there.

The signal she and the others were following, a low hum, grew louder. They were in the foothills. Josepha saw a glint of metal through the trees up ahead.

They came to another clearing and circled it, focusing on the signal. The robot Josepha had sent out waited there. The signal hummed in short bursts, telling her that the children were here. But they saw no one; only the signs, once again, of a campfire.

They dropped quickly to the ground. Josepha landed clumsily, stumbling onto her hands and knees. Alf helped her to her feet.

The Renewal

"I don't understand it," Gurit said as she strode around the clearing, peering at the trees, searching the ground for signs. Her middle-aged face was tense with worry; the lines near her lips were deep. Josepha waited unsteadily, still feeling unbalanced by the jet. Gurit stopped, bent over, then stood up. She held something in her hand.

She came back to Josepha and Alf, holding out the object. "Look, a Bond bracelet."

"I don't understand," Alf murmured.

"Very clever," Gurit said.

"But we should be getting signals from the other Bonds, shouldn't we?" Josepha shook her head, bewildered.

"This is a tricky business," Gurit replied. "Someone has relayed the signals through this one device and has managed to do it without triggering any emergency alert systems. I wouldn't know how to begin doing that."

"Then how," Alf said, his trembling voice betraying his fear, "are we going to find them?"

"The computer can track them if we turn off this Bond," Gurit said, "assuming, of course, that no one's fooled with the other Bonds."

"You think the children could have done this?"

Gurit looked from Alf to Josepha. "Possibly. I don't know why they would."

Josepha felt sick and cold, as if the weather had suddenly changed. "What should we do, Gurit?"

"We can go back home, put the computer to work, send robots out to search, and request a satellite scan of the entire area, but that might take days." She paused. "Or we can keep searching."

"But we don't know where . . ." Josepha began.

"I have an idea," Gurit interrupted. "Don't get scared when I tell you this. There was a landslide near here four days ago after that severe storm we had. My computer mentioned it after the storm was over, but I didn't think about it, I was sure the children had found shelter or else . . ." Gurit gazed guiltily down at her feet. Josepha knew what she was thinking: all of them had relied too much on the machines to guard the children. "They may be trapped," Gurit finished. She did not mention the other possibilities.

"That settles it, then," Alf said. "We must look for them near the landslide." His voice quavered.

A hill of dirt and rocks stood before them.

"There was a cave here, I think," Gurit murmured. "They might have gone inside during the storm." She removed her jet as she spoke, dropping it on the ground with a soft thud. She hurried to the mound and began to climb carefully.

Josepha reached for Alf's hand. She was numb, imagining Teno entombed inside, without food, without air. They could live without the food, but air . . . She thought: nature has killed them because they're mutants, travesties—and it wants to let us know that we can still die here, that nothing can protect us forever. She recalled the frequent trips of the young people from the village, their attempts to understand the natural world that was part of them and yet outside them.

Alf gripped her hand tightly, and she realized she would be hysterical if she gave in to her thoughts. Alf's hand was sweaty, his delicate face frozen. His blue eyes were filled with fear. He leaned against her heavily; she put her arms around him and his jet.

She watched quietly as Gurit scrambled over the rocks near the top of the mound. Gurit fell to her knees and did not move. Josepha waited, wondering what the woman had seen.

Then Gurit stood. "There's an opening here," she shouted down. Josepha sighed; the young people could not have suffocated. Gurit was bending over again.

"Do you hear something?" Josepha asked Alf, sure she was imagining the sound of another voice. Alf shook his head.

"They're inside," Gurit cried. She sat down suddenly at the top of the hill. "Call for help, they're inside."

Josepha had expected Chane to be angry, to reproach her and the other parents for their lack of supervision or to turn his wrath on the children. Instead, he had silently thrown his arms around Ramli, then Teno.

She had wanted to question the children about the reasons for their actions. But Teno and Ramli had been too tired to do more than bathe and eat a few raw vegetables before going to sleep. Chane's journey home had wearied him as well. The accounting would have to take place the next day.

She entered the living room. Chane was sitting on the sofa smoking a cigarette. She sat down next to him and touched his hand gently. He did not speak.

Most of the village had gathered near the cave that afternoon, waiting as the robots dug, sighing and crying when the young people finally emerged. Merripen, standing near Josepha, had unexpectedly hugged her when he saw the children.

The children were tired and dirty but seemed to have few injuries. Three medical robots had treated the cuts and bruises while protein tablets and water were distributed and adults hurried to the young people. Josepha had waited with Teno and Ramli for the hovercrafts that would take them all home.

Both children had been remarkably calm, describing some of their ordeal in steady voices. They had been trapped after taking shelter from the storm. After discovering that air could still reach them, they had parceled out the few provisions they had. Aided by the glow of their portable lanterns, they had tried to repair a Bond in order to signal for help.

"We shorted out four Bonds," Teno said quietly. "It's not that easy to repair them after fooling with them. By then a few lanterns had given out and we had to conserve the rest. I was making some progress with my Bond when Gurit came."

It was impossible for her to tell if they had been frightened at all. She gazed at them, trying to discern some difference, then saw one; neither child would look at her directly. "We made a mistake, rigging the Bonds," Ramli said.

"Why did you do it then?"

"We were sure you wouldn't worry about us, and we didn't want others to find us. You know some don't wish us well."

"You could have died." Instantly Josepha wished that she had not spoken so harshly.

"I know. We all thought we might. We didn't want to."

They had said little more on the way home.

"Don't be sad," Josepha said now to Chane. He tried to smile, but his dark eyes remained morose. "They're safe, and maybe they've learned something from all of this, something we couldn't have taught. I'll admit, it's learning things the hard way, but—"

"They've learned they can die," he responded. "And before that, when Nenum was killed, they learned they might have to hide. Do you think those are useful lessons,

The Renewal

Josepha?" She did not reply. "They have learned fear."

"I don't know if they have or not, I couldn't tell."

"And they may react the way many of us have, by retreating."

"Is something else bothering you, Chane?"

He put out his cigarette and lit another, passing the box to her. "I will tell you something you won't find in any public record of my life," he said suddenly. "Do you want to hear it? It's not pleasant."

She lit her cigarette. "If you want to tell it, I'll listen."

"You know that during the Transition I was in hiding. I trusted only two people with information about where I was. I wanted to live until it was over and like many in public life I had enemies. A friend contacted me, one of those I trusted. He pleaded with me to return to the capitol, another government had fallen and he wanted me to help form another, they needed my foreign contacts and experience. As you may know, some countries managed to restore civil order before many African countries could. He thought they might help. As an additional incentive, he told me that my wife and one of my children were imprisoned, prisoners of a tribe sometimes hostile to my own. He was trying to get them and others released but needed my aid."

Josepha waited for him to continue, tapping her ashes into a pewter tray. Chane was hunched over, elbows on knees, staring down at his feet. "I didn't go," he said at last, so softly she could barely hear him. "It was too risky, I thought, telling myself I couldn't have done much anyway. I didn't go. I hid. In fact, I moved so that no one could contact me again."

She had to say something. She reached toward him, then pulled her arm back. "But," she began. She swallowed.

"You said," she went on, "that your wife and children were still alive."

"They are. Does that make me any less culpable? Do you want to know what she went through during her imprisonment? Her body was repaired and her mind was wiped of the experience afterward, but I am still a witness to it, I was told everything. I will never have it wiped from my memory. That is part of my punishment."

She stubbed out her cigarette. He moved away from her and slouched at the other end of the sofa. "I have wanted to redeem myself since then if I could. That's why I came here and it is also why I left after Nenum's death. At least that's what I thought at the time—I wanted to stay here, but I thought speaking to others was more important. Maybe it was just an excuse to retreat from you."

"Why didn't you tell me this before?"

"Don't you see? At first I didn't think I knew you well enough, and later . . . I couldn't tell how you felt toward me. You never even argued with me very much."

She sat up. "Why should I have argued with you?"

"It would have shown you cared."

"I thought trying to be rational and pleasant was a better way of showing care. There isn't very much worth arguing about when you know sooner or later it'll be forgotten."

He sighed. "That sounds like selfishness, not concern."

"Why?"

He rose and paced to the window, then turned to face her. "It keeps you from getting involved, from committing yourself. I know, I'm guilty of the same thing. Why didn't you get angry over Warner?"

Josepha opened her mouth to speak, but Chane continued. "Because you would have had to admit your pain and maybe that it was partly your fault as well. Why did I do it? Maybe in some way I was testing you, Josepha. Why didn't you do the same thing? Because you could make me feel guilty by not retaliating, yet avoid any real confrontation where we might have had to make a decision one way or another."

"But I love you," she said, feeling the words were almost useless. "I have for a while. What you did long ago doesn't matter to me now. All of us did things like that or we wouldn't be alive today." She paused, then forced herself to continue. "I worked for a shady cryonic service, even though I suspected many of their clients would never be revived. I bought longevity shots illegally. I didn't do much to make anyone's life better. And before that, out of fear, I ran away from the only man I ever really loved, and when I was an adolescent, I tried to run away through suicide."

"I guess," Chane replied. "that we have at last laid our cards on the table. We humans are peculiar, aren't we? I can see why Merripen wanted a change."

She stood up. "What do we do now, Chane?"

He crossed the room and put an arm around her. "We settle things with Teno and Ramli, between ourselves, and then . . ." He paused. "Right now, I think we need rest."

The children, Josepha noticed, looked almost guilty. They poked at their bananas and milk, gazing obliquely at her and Chane across the table.

"You caused us a lot of pain and worry," Chane began. "I want to know the reasons."

"Chane," Josepha said hesitantly, "can't we wait until we've finished breakfast first?"

"No."

"We made a mistake," Teno said softly. "We needed to be alone for a while, we had some things to work out and decisions to make."

"Couldn't you have made your decisions here?" Chane asked.

"We had to be by ourselves. We didn't think you would worry and we wanted to make sure no one hostile to us knew where we were."

"But you could have gone to the lodges," Josepha said. "You could have had robots protect you there."

Teno stared directly at her. "That didn't help Nenum."

"We're sorry," Ramli said. "Maybe we should have told you. We thought you'd have more trust in us. We forgot that you don't see things quite the way we do. And we didn't count on an accident, though we should have. We were too busy protecting ourselves from other people."

They were trying to twist it around, Josepha thought, trying to make it their fault. It should not have surprised her; quite naturally the young people thought themselves more rational than their parents. "Have you decided anything?" she asked.

"We had to decide," Teno said calmly, "whether to stay here, voluntarily exile ourselves, or pursue a third course."

"Wait a minute," Chane interrupted. "Don't you think your parents have anything to say about what you're going to do?"

"Please let me finish," Teno replied tonelessly. "You were right when you decided to speak to people outside the village and to have more visitors here. The problem is that you didn't go far enough. We need to live with other people now. Maybe we should have been brought up with other children from the beginning. We want to move away from here. It will be hard—I don't know how well we'll get along, but we have to start."

"You want us to build another village somewhere else?" Chane said.

The Renewal

"No," Teno responded. "That would be the same thing we have now. We want to live with others. Some of us may live off-planet, the others in different societies here. It won't be easy, having to leave each other, but it's the only way. People won't see us as a group then, but as individuals. And we'll be forced to learn, to get along, to find out what to do, each of us, because we won't have the others to lean on. Instead of isolating ourselves, we'll learn how we can help."

"But you're so young," Josepha said, looking to Chane for support. "You're children, you don't know what you're doing. You can't decide something like that yet."

"We're not like you, Josepha," her child said. "We don't have much experience, but that doesn't make us children. Physically, we're grown. We don't have the hormonal changes and emotional problems others do at our age."

"It's time for us to lead our own lives," Ramli added.

"And what are we to do?" Chane said, sounding weary. "Go with you? Stay here? Do what we want? Did you think of us at all?"

"Do what you think is best," Ramli said. It sounded cold to Josepha; the child seemed to realize that. "We're not abandoning you," Ramli went on. "You'll see us often, you can advise us. You'll have to tell us if we're doing something wrong."

Josepha, looking at the two serious young faces, knew that they and the others would have their way, whatever the parents or Merripen or anyone else thought. The children would take their leave; she and Chane would have their own decisions to make. They would leave the village; there would be no point in remaining. It all reminded her of death, the end of one thing, the beginning of another.

5

The autumn leaves, bright spots of orange, red, and yellow, covered the ground near the creek. They rustled under the feet of Josepha and Teno, muffling the cracks of dead twigs. Overhead, sunlight shrouded by gray clouds penetrated the webbing of bare tree limbs.

Teno, clothed in sweat pants and a heavy red jacket, walked with hands shoved into pockets. The child's gray eyes matched the cloudy sky and seemed to hide as much. "I'll call you from Asgard," Teno was saying. "I may go to the Moon afterward."

"I've never been off Earth," Josepha murmured. "It seems silly now, sort of unenterprising."

"Maybe you'll visit me," her child said. "Isn't it about time you went?"

"Probably. I hope I can bring myself to set foot in a shuttle."

"The future may be there. We talked about it, all of us. We want to find out more. We're curious, I think we'll go on a long journey someday, or our descendants will. They probably won't be anything like you or ourselves."

"Probably not."

"Even we might not be the same. We've talked about somatic changes, readjustments in our bodies, but I think we'll need more experience before deciding what to do."

They turned from the creek and walked back toward the house. The old maple tree still remained; the apple tree Josepha had planted still lived, although its fruit was small and bitter. The house itself looked the same but felt old, unused, musty. She had left the village hoping to gain some strength from her old home and had felt only displaced. She could no longer live here.

"Will you go live with Chane, Josepha?"

"Yes, at least for a while. He wants me to travel with him, meet some of his friends. He feels he has to continue speaking for you. He's probably right."

"He is right. Our plans may not work out. Some call us infiltrators—as if we're subversive." Teno sniffed loudly. "It's good that you'll be with Chane. Without Ramli and me to worry about all the time, you'll be able to work things out between you."

Josepha stopped and turned to her child, gazing into Nicholas Krol's gray eyes. "Teno," she said hesitantly, "there's one thing I have to ask, it may seem strange or silly to you, but humor me for a bit." She paused. "I don't know how to put it exactly. Do you have any feelings for me at all, as a parent? Do you really, deep down, feel any sort of an attachment, any concern? I just want to know."

The gray, quiet eyes watched her calmly. "It would be strange," the child answered, "if we could have lived among you without coming to some understanding of your feelings. Of course I'm concerned. I care about you and I'd feel a loss if I no longer saw you or couldn't speak to you. If one loses a friend or companion, one loses another perspective, another viewpoint, a different set of ideas and the personality that has formed them."

"That isn't quite what I meant." Josepha struggled with the words. "Do you feel any love?" She waited, wondering what Teno thought.

Teno was silent for a few moments. Josepha thought: I shouldn't have asked. A person could profess love, but actions were what counted. Teno and the others had tried to show all the love they were capable of feeling if they could feel it at all. One could not ask, should not ask.

"Do you believe," Teno said softly, "that only your physiology, your glands, your hormones can produce love? It isn't true. Love is part of a relationship, it can't be reduced to physical characteristics or body chemistry. I love you, Josepha. I'll care about you as long as I know you or remember you."

She should not have asked. The words could tell her nothing. She could still doubt, still wonder if the child was telling her what would be most comforting.

But Teno's face was changing. As she watched, she saw the child's lips form a crescent, and realized with a shock that Teno was smiling. It was a slow smile, a gentle smile, compassionate but impenetrable. A softness seemed to flicker behind the gray eyes. It was Teno's parting gift.

The smile too might be a comforting mask. But as she entered the house with her child, Josepha decided she would accept it.